UNMARKED GRAVES

The car was now less than five hundred yards from the high, barbed-wire-topped fence that formed a barrier between the speeding Mercedes and the runway beyond.

The tall, heavy-lidded man in the back seat sat motionless, his eyes scanning the troops who had taken up position behind an army truck close to the fence. Every now and then he looked beyond them to the Cessna.

Three hundred yards.

A bullet struck the windscreen of the Mercedes.

The glass spider-webbed but the driver merely leaned forward and punched a hole through it. Warm air and dust rushed in.

The man in the passenger seat tightened his finger round the trigger of the Kalashnikov, raking the troops ahead. The assault rifle bucked venomously in his hand and it was all he could do to keep the weapon steady as the recoil shook it. Empty shell cases sprayed into the air and all over the car.

Two hundred yards.

By Shaun Hutson

Assassin
Body Count
Breeding Ground
Captives
Compulsion
Deadhead
Death Day
Dying Words
Erebus
Exit Wounds
Heathen
Hell to Pay
Hybrid
Knife Edge
Lucy's Child
Necessary Evil
Nemesis
Purity
Relics
Renegades
Shadows
Slugs
Spawn
Stolen Angels
Twisted Souls
Unmarked Graves
Victims
Warhol's Prophecy
White Ghost

Shaun Hutson Omnibus 1
Shaun Hutson Omnibus 2

SHAUN HUTSON

UNMARKED GRAVES

www.orbitbooks.net

ORBIT

First published in Great Britain in 2007 by Orbit
This paperback edition published in 2008 by Orbit

Copyright © Shaun Hutson 2007

Excerpt from *Already Dead*
Copyright © 2005 by Charlie Huston

A CIP catalogue record for this book
is available from the British Library.

ISBN 978-1-84149-436-4

Typeset in Bembo by Palimpsest Book Production Limited,
Grangemouth, Stirlingshire
Printed in the UK by CPI Mackays, Chatham ME5 8TD

Papers used by Orbit are natural, renewable and recyclable
products made from wood grown in sustainable forests and certified
in accordance with the rules of the Forest Stewardship Council.

Mixed Sources
Product group from well-managed
forests and other controlled sources
www.fsc.org Cert no. SGS-COC-004081
© 1996 Forest Stewardship Council

FSC

Orbit
An imprint of
Little, Brown Book Group
100 Victoria Embankment
London EC4Y 0DY

An Hachette Livre UK Company
www.hachettelivre.co.uk

www.orbitbooks.net

This book is dedicated to my mum and dad.
With love and thanks.

Acknowledgements

As ever, the following list is of people, places and things that have featured in my life in some significant (or trivial!) way before, during or after the writing of this novel.

I extend a big thank you to everyone mentioned. The reasons why those thanks are merited, the people in question ought to know.

To the following people at my publishers: Barbara Daniel, Darren Nash, Andy Edwards, Carol Donnelly and my 'Wild Bunch'.

To my agent, Brie Burkeman, to Isabelle and to everyone at the Buckman agency.

Special thanks again to Stephane Marsan at Bragelonne in France.

To James Whale (and Melinda). To Ash.

To Bruce Jones and Shane Richie.

Thanks also go out to October 11 Pictures. Jason Figgis, Maria Figgis and Jonathan Figgis.

Jo Roberts and Gatlin pictures.

Rod Smallwood, Val Janes and Dave Pattenden at Sanctuary (or should that be Phantom) music.

Steve, Dave, Bruce, Adrian, Janick and Nicko.

Marc Shemmans.

Ian Austin, Zena, Terri, Becky and Rachel, Nicky.

Brian at the bank. Leslie and Sue Tebbs. Everyone at Chancery.

Martin Phillips.

Graeme Sayer and Callum Hughes.

A special thank you to Cineworld UK, especially Mr Al Alvarez and to everyone at Cineworld Milton Keynes. To Mark Johnson, Martin, Mel, Debbie, Paula, Terry, Dave (who tried to kill me one Monday . . .) Kim and Keira and anyone else I've forgotten or who's left by now . . .

Liverpool football club. Aaron Reynolds (who puts up with more than most during the drives . . .). Steve Lucas. Paul Garner. Everyone who sits around me inside Anfield. Neil Davies and his wonderful family, Tommy, Dave, Pete, Kev, Brian, Paul and Phil.

Incredible thanks to my mum and dad. As ever and forever.

The thanks I owe my wife, Belinda, are beyond measure as is my love and admiration for her.

That goes for my fantastic daughter too. I wish I had a tenth of her focus, courage and determination. She must get it from her mum . . .

As ever, the last thanks goes to my readers. You're always there and I hope you always will be. Long may it continue.

Let's go.

Shaun Hutson

'What survives myself? The brazen statue to o'erlook my grave, set on the promontory I named.'

Robert Browning

Marabana, twenty-seven miles east of Freetown, Sierra Leone, West Africa

With the head severed, it was hard to guess the age of the corpse that lay in the bath.

In fact, so savage were the mutilations that had been performed on the rest of the body, a quick glance didn't even immediately disclose its sex.

However, closer inspection would reveal that the body was female. Despite the fact that both breasts had been hacked off, there was enough of the ravaged mammary tissue left to testify to that.

The genital area had also been subjected to extensive butchery. Seven deep gashes, two of which had torn open the inside of the left thigh, had turned the area between the dead woman's legs into little more than a blood-choked hole. Portions of the severed vaginal lips lay in the bottom of the bath like strips of raw steak.

The cracked enamel of the bath was coated with

blood, as were the walls and floor of the bathroom. Great crimson arcs of arterial spray had spattered everywhere. Some of the red liquid had begun to congeal. The room looked and smelled like a slaughterhouse.

Splashes of blood led through into the bedroom. The floor there was bare wood and the red fluid had, in places, begun to seep into the porous material. The room was lit by the glow of more than two dozen candles, most of them arranged on the small wooden bedside cabinet and the bed itself. The pungent odour of blood mingled with the smell of burning wax.

And there was another odour too that helped to clog the air in the bedroom. It was the smell of human sweat.

Killing and slaughtering the girl had required more effort than was desirable in temperatures of over one hundred degrees.

The hotel room was barely cooled by a ceiling fan that turned slowly like the upturned rotor blades of a helicopter, doing little to affect the cloying heat. It served only to mix the array of odours that permeated the almost unbreathable air.

The tall man who knelt naked at the foot of the bed murmured quiet words and kept his gaze fixed on the severed head propped between candles on the pillows wedged against the wall. Beads of sweat ran down his face and his upper body, but he seemed neither to care nor to notice. He was content to continue mouthing words, his lips moving quickly, his heavy-lidded brown gaze never leaving the open eyes of the head he himself had cut from the girl's body barely thirty minutes earlier.

The machete he'd used for the task lay close by him on the floor of the hotel bedroom. As well as the blood that covered the metal, there were small pieces of flesh on the cutting edge of the blade.

'*Kadiempembe.*'

He spoke that one word softly, almost reverently. Then he lowered his head until his chin touched his sweat-slicked chest and closed his eyes.

The severed head regarded him indifferently, the dull glow of the candles reflected in the sightless, glassy orbs.

'*Kadiempembe.*'

He raised his head a fraction and reached for the machete, gripping the handle in one large hand. He turned the blade towards his chest and pressed the cold metal gently against his flesh just below his left nipple. Murmuring something unintelligible under his breath, he prepared to cut.

He heard heavy footfalls on the stairs and then a noise outside the hotel room. He turned his head. Hesitant voices were audible outside the door and then came three hard bangs on the flimsy wooden partition.

The man gripped the machete tighter in his fist, the muscles at the side of his jaw pulsing angrily.

The door swung open.

There were two men standing there. Both were holding AK-47 assault rifles.

'We must go,' the first said, urgently, seemingly unperturbed by what he saw inside the hotel room.

Still holding the machete, the man in the room rose slowly, unconcerned by his own nakedness. He looked at each of the two armed men then nodded almost imperceptibly. However, he did not move from the end of the bed.

The second man dashed back down the stairs, the Kalashnikov gripped tightly in his fists.

'There is no more time,' the first armed man insisted breathlessly. 'They are coming.'

1

Bermondsey, South London, England

Nick Pearson sipped tea from the plastic cup and looked at the gun.

It was an HK81 rifle. Manufactured by Heckler und Koch in Germany, it held a magazine of thirty 7.62mm rounds and was capable of unleashing eight hundred shots a minute.

But not today, Pearson thought as he watched the armed policemen peering through the telescopic sights mounted on the weapons. On this particular day, these guns would be used as sniper rifles. Precision was the key in this situation.

Just as it was wherever hostages were involved.

'You should move further back. I've told you once.'

The voice came from behind him and Pearson turned to see a powerfully built man dressed in a grey suit walking towards him.

'If matey boy in there starts shooting,' went on

the grey-suited man, inclining his head towards the house across the street, 'Christ knows what he'll hit.'

'We'll be OK, Detective Inspector,' Pearson assured him. 'But thanks for your concern.'

'I'm not concerned about your health,' the policeman told him. 'I just don't want you lot getting in the way if we have to go in. If one of you gets hit by a stray bullet, it'll mean more paperwork for somebody. Probably me.'

Pearson smiled. 'We've been in these situations before.'

'Yeah, I know you have,' the DI said.

'What's he asking for?' Pearson enquired, hooking a thumb towards the house behind him. 'What are his demands?'

'He wants money. If he doesn't get it he'll kill them all. Pretty simple. He's out of his head on drugs – probably not even sure what day of the week it is.'

'That's his wife and kids in there with him, isn't it?' Pearson took another sip of his tea. 'The boy's six and the girl's two. Can you confirm that?'

The policeman nodded.

'Is the negotiator talking to him at the moment?' Pearson continued.

'No one's talking to him,' the DI said flatly. 'He said if anyone came within fifty yards of the house he'd start shooting.'

'What kind of gun is he carrying?'

'An automatic.'

6

'Any idea where he got it?'

'They're not hard to come by if you know where to look. He obviously knew.'

'Has the entire street been evacuated?'

The DI signalled assent. 'The back's covered too,' he went on. 'There's no way out of there.'

From the corner of his eye, Pearson saw a uniformed man hurrying towards the detective. In front of him, two more armed men were taking up position behind a parked car.

'Can I talk to you, sir?' the uniformed man said, glancing first at Pearson, then at his camera man and sound operator.

The detective nodded agreement and guided the man away from the watching news team. Pearson took another sip of tea as he watched them go.

'May as well get some more coverage of the street while we're waiting, Bill,' he said, watching as the camera man panned slowly up and down Banyard Road.

'Do you reckon he'll kill them, Nick?' the sound man asked conversationally.

'He's a smackhead,' Pearson muttered. 'He's scared. He's angry and he's got a gun. I wouldn't want to be in there with him, would you?'

The sound man shook his head.

'I'll bet you a fiver he shoots them all then tops himself,' the camera man offered. He dug a hand into his jeans and pulled out a five pound note. 'Who's in?'

Pearson reached for his wallet and flipped it open. 'He'll kill his missus, then the police will shoot him,' the reporter said.

Both of them turned towards the sound man.

'Coppers get him before he shoots anyone,' he said, producing money of his own.

Pearson finished his tea and looked towards the house across the street.

'Let's see, shall we?' he murmured.

Lokobento, two miles east of Lungi Airport, Sierra Leone, West Africa

Dust sprayed up on either side of the speeding Mercedes like waves in the wake of a motorboat.

The car bumped and thudded over the narrow and holed dirt road, scraping its axles on more than one occasion. But the driver kept control of the vehicle, his foot pressed hard to the accelerator, his gaze fixed ahead.

The road looked clear.

In the back seat, two men with Kalashnikovs sat on either side of the tall man with the heavy-lidded eyes, one of them glancing anxiously out of the rear window. The tall man seemed unconcerned and merely peered ahead, past the driver and the man in the passenger seat, who held another Kalashnikov.

In the golden glow of the rising sun, the tall man could see the countryside stretching away from him on all sides. Scrubby outcrops of short grass pushed up through the dust and sand and, here and there, a stunted tree lifted skeletal branches towards the sky but, otherwise, there was no sign of life in this barren wilderness.

Nocturnal hunters had already retreated back to their lairs with the appearance of the sun. The daylight would bring only the most hardy of creatures out into the open to face temperatures that would soar above one hundred and ten degrees in the shade.

The heat was already intensifying as the sun continued to climb above the horizon, staining the earth with its incandescent gold and red hues and tinting the sparse early morning wisps of cloud like ink seeping into blotting paper.

The man in the passenger seat worked the bolt on his Kalashnikov, chambering a round. The metallic rattle reverberated inside the Mercedes.

'The plane will be waiting,' he said, turning briefly to look at the tall man. 'We will get you as close as we can.'

The tall man nodded slowly.

'They will not catch you,' one of the men in the back seat with him said. 'We will not allow that.'

The driver pressed down harder on the accelerator, urging the car up a slight rise. He swerved to avoid a large rock in the road then drove on, cresting the ridge.

Ahead, off to the right of the road, was a collection of dwellings and the tall man could see people moving about among them. A child, no more than ten, was herding half a dozen goats across the dry ground, but where he was going to find food for them only he knew.

The rising sun cast its burnished glow over the collection of huts and their residents, many of whom peered inquisitively in the direction of the speeding Mercedes.

'How long?' the man in the passenger seat asked, glancing at the driver.

'Thirty minutes,' the driver told him, his eyes never leaving the road.

'The plane will wait until we arrive,' the man in the passenger seat said, turning again to look at the tall man. 'It will not leave without you.'

The tall man moved in his seat, gazing ahead.

The Mercedes accelerated, the needle of the speedometer touching seventy.

The rising sun, blazing fiercely as it continued its climb into the heavens, caused the driver to squint as it caught the rear-view mirror. He muttered something under his breath and reached for the sunglasses that lay beside the gear stick.

He was about to push them on to his face when the side window of the car exploded inwards.

2

Bermondsey, South London, England

Nick Pearson glanced at his watch and then dug in his jacket pocket for his cigarettes. He lit one and leaned back against the bonnet of a car, gazing across the street at No. 33 Banyard Road.

It was as unremarkable in appearance as the other houses in the thoroughfare. Some of them had fake stone cladding, most sported satellite dishes, but other than that they were relatively uniform.

'How long have we been here now?' his sound man asked. 'Three hours? Longer?'

'You know this kind of job involves a lot of waiting around, Mike,' Pearson remarked, drawing on his cigarette.

'Yeah, but I do it because I have to. You could be tucked up in some nice cosy studio somewhere, Nick. Not out here with us mere mortals.'

All three of them laughed.

'I'm still a reporter,' Pearson reminded him. 'I'd

rather be out and about working on stories than sitting behind a desk reading them.'

He heard the sound of an engine to his right and looked round to see an ambulance pulling into position beside a police van.

'I wonder how long it'll be before they need that?' Pearson nodded in the direction of the ambulance.

'Not as warm here as it was on your last assignment, I'll bet,' the sound man offered.

Pearson smiled. 'No,' he agreed. 'If my dad hadn't died I'd probably still be in Africa now.'

'Shit, I'm sorry,' the sound man apologised. 'I'd forgotten about your dad.'

'Don't worry about it,' Pearson said. 'Life goes on and all that.' He took another drag on his cigarette.

'Your dad wasn't in TV, was he, Nick?' the camera man enquired.

'No,' Pearson told him. 'He had more sense. He was a plumber all his life. He thought I was mad when I said I wanted to work in the business. He said I should get a proper job.' A gust of cold wind swept along the street and Pearson turned up the collar of his jacket. 'Maybe he was right.'

'You worked in Iraq, didn't you?' the sound man asked.

'Iraq. Afghanistan. Kosovo. But mainly Africa and no, that isn't just because I'm black and they thought I'd blend in.'

All three men laughed once more.

Pearson took a final drag on his cigarette then dropped the butt and ground it out with his shoe.

'Anybody want another cup of tea?' he asked. 'I'm going to wander down to that burger van at the end of the road.'

Armed with the other men's orders, the reporter set off along the pavement towards the far end of Banyard Road, passing marked and unmarked police cars and vans as he went. Some had men inside. Most were being used as cover by the armed officers hunkering behind them, their rifles aimed at the windows of No. 33.

He could see several communicating by two-way radio and mobile phone. One of the marksmen was adjusting his telescopic sight. Focusing.

How much longer?

Pearson's mobile phone began to ring.

Lungi Airport, Sierra Leone, West Africa

The bullet that had blasted in the side window of the Mercedes had missed the driver by inches.

The man in the passenger seat had not been so lucky.

The high velocity round had caught him in the right shoulder, drilling into the flesh and muscle with ease and almost shattering the top of the humerus. Now he sat stiffly in his seat, face contorted with pain, gazing ahead to the dusty runway that was less than a thousand yards away.

The airport control tower rose high above the terminal buildings, thrusting upwards like a finger as if pointing the way for the planes that were waiting on the runway.

As the Mercedes drew nearer, the men inside the vehicle could clearly see four planes on the long stretch of tarmac ahead of them. One was an old, rusted Russian cargo plane that was already beginning to taxi, its four large propellers spinning ever more quickly. A small green-painted passenger craft had a gantry pushed up to its forward exit doors although there was no sign of people either boarding or disembarking, and two private planes also stood on the tarmac.

It was to the larger of these that the driver pointed.

'There,' he said excitedly, his finger indicating a white Cessna U-27A.

As he spoke he saw several uniformed figures spreading out from the front of the airport's main building.

'Government troops,' the man in the passenger seat said, wincing from the pain in his shoulder as he thrust the AK-47 out of the window and held it in one powerful fist.

The driver gripped the wheel more tightly and floored the accelerator.

The car was now less than five hundred yards from the high, barbed-wire-topped fence that formed a barrier between the speeding Mercedes and the runway beyond.

The tall, heavy-lidded man in the back seat sat motionless, his eyes scanning the troops who had taken up position behind an army truck close to the fence. Every now and then he looked beyond them to the Cessna.

Three hundred yards.

A bullet struck the windscreen of the Mercedes. The glass spider-webbed but the driver merely leaned forward and punched a hole through it. Warm air and dust rushed in.

The man in the passenger seat tightened his finger round the trigger of the Kalashnikov, raking the troops ahead. The assault rifle bucked venomously in his hand and it was all he could do to keep the weapon steady as the recoil shook it. Empty shell cases sprayed into the air and all over the car.

Two hundred yards.

Another round hit the radiator grille of the Mercedes. Two more blasted away the front head-lights. The driver turned the wheel frantically to left and right, causing the vehicle to swerve first one way then the other.

One hundred yards.

Bullets from the waiting soldiers hit the oncoming car, either screaming off the chassis or blasting holes in the bodywork. One sent the remains of the left wing mirror spinning into the air.

The two men in the back of the car flanking the tall man now began to fire as well and streams of 7.62mm ammo, moving at a speed in excess of 2,300 feet a second, began to cut into the uniformed men guarding the perimeter fence. Several fell, one screaming in agony and clutching what remained of his face.

On the runway ahead, the Cessna began to move slowly down the dusty tarmac.

The car driver gripped the wheel with both hands and ducked his head.

The Mercedes smashed into the wire fence and tore through with ease, ripping two of the fence posts from the ground in its wake. Bullets drilled into the car, one bursting the rear off-side tyre, another staving in the rear windscreen and catching one of the men in the back seat.

The bullet powered into the base of his skull and exploded from his mouth, severing his spinal cord and killing him instantly. Blood, pulverised bone and slivers of flesh spattered the occupants of the Mercedes.

The other man in the back seat turned his Kalashnikov and fired through the smashed window, emptying the thirty-round magazine in seconds as the car skidded on to the runway and sped towards the Cessna.

The plane slowed almost to a halt as the Mercedes drew alongside it and the surviving guard in the back seat clambered out, using the vehicle as cover while he returned the sporadic fire of the troops, some of whom started running across the tarmac until the ferocity of the fire being directed at them and the lack of cover forced them back.

The tall man scrambled from the back of the car and dashed towards the open door of the Cessna. He hauled himself in and immediately the aircraft began to speed up, gathering pace until it was hurtling down the runway.

Behind him, the second guard fell to the ground and lay twitching in a spreading pool of blood.

Two bullets struck the hull of the plane, whining off the metal as the tall man strapped himself into his seat, the perspiration pouring down his face.

'Hold on,' shouted the pilot as the Cessna reached its take-off speed, the single Pratt and Whitney turbo-prop roaring.

The plane left the ground and began climbing high into the cloudless sky, rising at over a thousand feet a minute.

'We're clear,' the pilot called, relieved.

The tall man relaxed back into his seat.

The Cessna cut across the sky, away from the airport.

It would be more than two hours before it touched down at its appointed destination.

3

Bermondsey, South London, England

'Pearson,' the reporter said, pressing his mobile to his ear.

'Nick, it's Gordon Dale,' the voice at the other end informed him. 'Anything happening?'

'Put the TV on and have a look,' Pearson told him.

'Yeah, very funny. Are you broadcasting live?'

'No, nothing's happening at the moment. The police have got the place surrounded. It's just a matter of who starts shooting first, them or the guy inside the house.'

'Why don't you come back to the studio so we can run over the rest of the stuff for the programme tonight? I'll send someone else over to cover that shit where you are.'

'I'm hoping to use some of this story in the programme tonight, Gordon.'

'Why, because the hostage taker's black?'

'The programme's about racial violence. What's your problem?'

'But this is different.'

'No it isn't. The hostage taker's black and his wife's white. In my book that's racial.'

At the other end of the phone, Dale sighed.

'Fair enough,' he conceded. 'I just think we've got enough material already and I need you to decide what goes in and what comes out.'

'I'm not leaving here yet, Gordon.'

Dale chuckled. 'Do you smell blood, Nick?'

'Maybe,' Pearson told him.

'Just watch yourself.'

'That's what the police told me.'

'I'll speak to you later,' Dale said and hung up.

Pearson slid his mobile back into his jacket pocket.

His nostrils were suddenly assaulted by the smell of strong coffee and cooking onions. He reached the burger van parked at the end of the street and took up position behind two uniformed policemen. They were watching as the man inside the van poured tea from a huge metal teapot into styrofoam cups.

One of them turned and glanced at Pearson, who nodded amiably.

'You're that bloke off the telly, aren't you?' the policeman said. 'That reporter.'

'One of them.' Pearson smiled. The courtesy wasn't returned.

'I saw that programme you did about suspects

who died in police custody,' the policeman continued.

'What did you think?'

'I thought it was bullshit. All the cases you picked on involved black suspects.'

'That's because more black suspects die in police custody than white ones.'

'Bollocks,' sneered the policeman, pushing past him.

Pearson ignored the remark and stepped up to the counter of the van.

'Two teas, a coffee and a cheeseburger please,' he said. 'Onions on the burger.'

The thin, ruddy-faced man behind the counter set about filling the order, while the two uniformed men walked slowly away from the van, the one who had spoken glancing back disdainfully at the reporter.

Pearson could hear them muttering under their breath and he was fairly sure the muted speech was about him.

Getting paranoid?

He heard the words 'interfering', 'black' and 'bastard'.

No. You're not paranoid. They are talking about you.

The reporter collected the drinks and the burger and headed off back up Banyard Road.

As he walked, he felt other eyes on him.

Tucat, southern Morocco

The inside of the truck smelled like an open sewer.

The tall man looked in at the occupants, regarding each one indifferently, then he let go of the dust flap on the rear of the vehicle.

'Get in,' said the driver, picking at a rotten tooth with one dirty nail. He hawked and spat.

The tall man hesitated, holding the driver in his piercing gaze.

'This was part of the bargain,' the driver insisted. 'This is how I will take you to Tangier. You and them.' He hooked a thumb in the direction of the truck. 'Once we are there, you're on your own. All of you.'

The tall man pulled the dust flap aside once more. He counted twenty-seven people in the back of the battered Scania: men, women and children of all ages, all of them dressed in filthy, sweat-stained clothes. Those nearest to him recoiled slightly, moving back into the gloom.

He picked out a woman holding a child close to her sagging breasts. The child was crying softly.

Hunger, the tall man guessed. And the effects of heat and dehydration. Several of the truck's occupants were slumped back against its side walls. Possibly asleep. Maybe dead. None of their fellow travellers seemed to care which.

The tall man released the tarpaulin and shook his head.

'Too proud to travel with them?' The driver grinned. 'They are no different from you. They want what you want. They are fleeing their country just as you are.'

The tall man reached slowly into the pocket of his trousers and pulled out a wad of money. The driver looked on with interest.

'Dollars,' he noted.

The tall man counted out one hundred dollars in twenties and pushed the rest of the wad back into his pocket. He held out the five notes towards the driver, who nodded.

'*Two* hundred,' he said, swatting away a fly that was buzzing around his head. 'That gets you a ride up front with me.'

The tall man hesitated for a moment, his eyes boring into the driver, who took a step back.

'I know who you are,' the Moroccan said quietly. 'You can afford it. It buys my silence too. There are many who would like to know where you are. Where you are going.'

The tall man said nothing.

'Two hundred,' the driver repeated, some of the bravado gone from his voice.

The tall man slid his hand back into his pocket and pulled out the money once again. He counted off five more twenty dollar bills and shoved them into the driver's sweaty palm.

'Get in the cab,' the Moroccan said.

The tall man walked round to the other side of the vehicle and hauled himself into the passenger seat, watching as the driver started the engine. The Scania pulled away, bumping over the uneven road as it picked up speed.

The tall man sat upright in his seat, gazing out through the windscreen.

Occasionally he would look at the Moroccan driver.

More than once, the tall man reached inside his jacket and touched the hilt of the knife he had hidden there.

He looked impassively at the driver again and wondered when the time would come for him to use it.

4

Bermondsey, South London, England

Trevor Moore was having trouble breathing.

His mouth was dry. His heart was thumping hard against his ribs. He felt as if his head had been pumped full of air.

From inside No. 33 Banyard Road he could see the armed policemen in the street outside.

'Just let us go, Trev. Please.'

The voice came from the other side of the small bedroom. A woman's voice, plaintive and imploring.

'Shut up,' Moore snapped, still gazing out of the window.

'At least let the kids go,' she said more insistently.

'I said shut it,' he rasped, turning towards her, the 9mm automatic clutched in his fist.

Melanie Moore was seated on the single bed clutching her children close to her.

She was twenty: five years younger than the man who stood opposite her with the gun. The man she'd lived with for the last five years. Her skin was sallow and its pallor showed up more vividly the redness around her eyes where she'd been crying. The skin on her arms was also white, like curdled milk, except at the crook of her left arm where it was marked with bruises and scabby red blotches.

'Let the kids go?' Moore hissed. 'Why should I? They're not even mine.'

She sniffed back more tears and held the five-year-old girl and the three-year-old boy more tightly.

'Of course they're yours,' she gasped.

'Daddy,' the little girl bleated tearfully.

'I'm not your fucking daddy,' Moore snarled. 'Tell them who is their fucking daddy. Or don't you even know any more, you cunt?'

He took a step towards the frightened trio on the bed, the gun waving before him, the muzzle yawning in Melanie's direction.

'You don't know, do you?' he grated. 'I know. I've heard things.'

'From who?'

'People have told me you were fucking around behind my back while I was inside.'

Melanie shook her head.

The little boy began to cry, clutching the thread-bare pink rabbit he held tight to his face. Melanie snaked her arm more tightly round the child to comfort him.

'It's all right, Troy,' she whispered. 'Daddy's just not feeling well.'

'I'm not his fucking daddy,' Moore exploded.

The sound seemed volcanic inside such a small room and both children jumped at the noise.

'You think what you want,' Melanie protested. 'But they're both yours.' She felt warm tears running down her cheeks. 'You can't fucking do this. It isn't right.'

'I can do whatever I fucking want,' Moore rasped, now only inches away from her. She felt his spittle shower her face.

He raised the gun and pressed the cold barrel to her forehead.

'Now you tell me who you were fucking while I was inside,' he hissed, 'or I'll blow your fucking head off.'

She closed her eyes so tightly white stars danced behind her eyelids.

'I wasn't fucking anyone,' she shouted back defiantly.

Moore grabbed the girl and pulled her free of Melanie's grip. The child screamed.

'Let her go,' Melanie shrieked.

Moore pressed the muzzle of the automatic to his daughter's face, the front sight grazing her soft skin.

'Now, you tell me who you've been fucking,' he said, his eyes glazed, 'or I'll kill her now.'

5

The gunshot came from inside No. 33 Banyard Road: a loud crack that reverberated in the air and died slowly on the breeze.

'Shit,' Pearson murmured. 'Sounds like he's started.'

He looked towards the house across the street, aware that both his companions were reacting to the sound in the way he would have expected. His camera man began filming the front of the building and his sound man lifted the boom microphone into the air to capture any other noises.

Pearson saw several of the armed policemen swing their rifles up into position. He could hear the hiss of two-way radios. Instructions were being passed back and forth over the airwaves.

'They're not moving in,' the sound man muttered, also watching the uniformed men.

Four had moved closer to the front door of the

house, but other than that there didn't appear to be any attempt under way to storm the building.

'One shot,' Pearson noted. 'Even if he *has* killed somebody, there's still two hostages left alive in there. The law aren't going to burst in and risk anyone else getting hurt. Not yet.' He glanced at the camera man. 'Leave it for now, Mike.'

He lit another cigarette and stood gazing raptly at the facade of No. 33 Banyard Road.

'The next one goes through her fucking head.'

Trevor Moore held up the 9mm automatic and looked in the direction of the hole he'd just blown in the wall of the bedroom. The thunderous retort of the pistol was still ringing in his ears. The blinding white of the muzzle flash was seared across his retina.

Motes of dust turned in the air as pieces of plaster fell from the wall, and the smell of cordite, gunpowder and oil formed an acrid aroma that stung his nostrils as it mingled with the dust.

A single spent brass shell case lay on the grubby carpet a foot away.

Melanie Moore and her two children were all crying.

'Now you fucking tell me what I want to hear,' Moore insisted.

He sniffed and wiped his nose with the back of his hand, his mood suddenly changing.

'You got any gear in the house?' he asked conversationally.

Melanie shook her head. 'I told you I hadn't when you first got here,' she gasped.

Moore crossed to the window and peered out. 'Fucking coppers everywhere,' he snapped.

'What do you expect?' she demanded. 'Please, Trevor, just let us go before anyone gets hurt.'

He stepped back quickly from the window, pulling the thin curtains across once again to hide what was happening inside the room from prying eyes outside.

'No one's going to get hurt if they do as I say.'

'They'll kill you,' she told him.

'Is that what you're hoping?' He stepped nearer to her.

Melanie shook her head and held on to her children, both of whom were still crying.

Moore looked at each of them in turn, then at their mother.

'Fucking bitch,' he said, under his breath.

He raised the pistol until it was level with her head.

Officer Lee Knott, positioned on the roof of the house opposite, steadied himself and took a deep breath.

His finger rested gently on the trigger of the HK81.

He spoke quietly into the radio-microphone attached to his headset.

'Jaguar Three,' he said, his eye never straying from the telescopic sight. 'I've got the suspect in full view. I have a shot.'

Silence except for some mild static.

'Stand by,' the voice in his ear said.

More static.

Officer Knott kept his right eye pressed to the telescopic sight.

The head of Trevor Moore was right in the middle of the cross-hairs.

'Suspect still in view,' Knott repeated. 'Jaguar Three, awaiting instructions.'

His finger pressed a little harder on the trigger of the rifle. His heart thudded faster against his ribs. He took another deep breath to calm himself and waited.

6

Darworth, Hertfordshire, England

'Fucking black bastards.'

Paul Duggan took a drag on his cigarette and glared at the two men as they passed his car.

He watched them cross the road towards the Work and Pensions building. Both of the men were in their early thirties, six or more years older than Duggan.

'Probably talking about how much fucking money they're going to get,' Duggan grunted. 'Cunts.'

He looked at his companion in the passenger seat. Raymond Carlton was busy sending a text message, his thumb moving with dizzying speed over the buttons of the mobile's keypad.

'I said, look at those fucking black cunts,' Duggan repeated.

'I heard what you said,' Carlton muttered without looking up.

'Well fucking answer me then,' Duggan snapped.

'I'm busy,' Carlton told him, still concentrating on the message he was sending.

'We were told to watch this place,' Duggan reminded him. 'See how many of them go in and out. See if it's the same ones.'

'I know what we were told,' Carlton murmured. 'That's what we're doing, isn't it?'

'*I* am. You're too busy texting that slag you were with last night.'

'She's not a slag. Her name's Nikki and you're just jealous because her mate told you to fuck off.'

'Probably fucking lesbians.' Duggan took a final drag on his cigarette then dropped it out of the open window of the Peugeot.

'Oh, no.' Carlton smiled. 'Nikki is definitely not a lesbian. Not after what we did last night.' He looked at Duggan and grinned.

'Whatever,' Duggan sneered, returning his attention to the building opposite.

'We've seen *him* before.'

The voice came from the back seat of the Peugeot.

'There,' Errol Lawler said, leaning forward and jabbing a finger in the direction of a slightly built black man entering the Work and Pensions building.

'I don't know how you can tell,' Duggan grunted. 'All fucking niggers look the same to me.'

'He's right,' Carlton said. 'I recognise that geezer.'

'I suppose *you* can spot them easier because your fucking old man was one, Errol.' Duggan laughed.

'Fuck you,' Lawler rasped. 'My old man was born here same as you, me and Ray.'

'He was still a nigger,' Duggan said disdainfully. 'And you've got nigger blood in you. You can see it.'

'He's got a point, Errol,' Carlton offered, smiling. 'You ain't exactly white, are you?'

'My mum was white, my fucking dad was black. What do you expect?' Lawler reminded them. 'That still don't make me a nigger, does it? I fucking hate the black bastards as much as you do. I fucking hated me old man. He was a cunt. He used to kick the shit out of me mum and me.' He pulled distractedly at a loose thread on the corner of the blanket that lay across the back seat.

'Did you ever find out where he went when he fucked off?' Duggan asked.

'No,' Lawler told him flatly. 'How the fuck would I know? I was ten when the cunt walked out. Fucking good riddance too. I hope he's dead.'

'So you reckon because your old man was born here that makes him different to these other bastards, then?' Carlton said.

'I told you,' Lawler persisted. 'His dad was from Jamaica but he was born here. That makes him English. Me too.'

'Fuck off,' Duggan grunted. 'There ain't no black in the Union Jack, send the fucking bastards back.' He laughed and looked at Lawler in the rear-view mirror. 'And the half-chats too. You ain't pure blood, my son.'

Lawler raised two fingers and slumped back in the seat.

'Two coming out,' Carlton said quietly, his eyes narrowing.

'What do you want to do?' Duggan asked.

'Follow them, like we were told,' Carlton said. 'You use the car. I'll tail them on foot.'

Duggan started the engine.

Up ahead, the two black men who had left the Work and Pensions building walked unconcernedly along the street, talking to one another, oblivious of those who watched them.

'We sorted?' Carlton said quietly, never taking his eyes from the black men ahead.

Lawler nodded and slid his hand under the blanket on the back seat, pushing it back slightly to reveal the handles of three baseball bats.

'When you going to ring him?' Duggan said, keeping his eyes on their quarry.

'Soon,' Carlton said, clambering out of the car.

The black men walked on.

'You know where to go,' Carlton said. 'If there's any change, I'll ring you, right?'

Duggan nodded.

Carlton dug his hands into his jacket pockets and, keeping a reasonable distance, set off after the black men.

7

Bermondsey, South London, England

'Jaguar Three, is the subject still in view?'

Officer Lee Knott heard the words through his earpiece.

'Yes, sir,' he answered.

'Have you got a clear shot?'

Knott pulled the HK81 more tightly into his shoulder and ensured that Trevor Moore's head was still dead centre in the cross-threads of the telescopic sight.

'Yes, sir,' he breathed.

'Take the shot,' the voice told him.

For a split second, Knott hesitated, unsure whether or not he'd heard the command clearly enough.

'Take the shot?' he echoed, his mouth suddenly dry.

'Do it,' the voice in his ear insisted.

Knott thought briefly about killing a man and how this was the first time he'd ever been called upon to use his skills in this way.

He tried to swallow but couldn't.

Just do it. Do your job.

'Take the shot,' the voice repeated.

Knott checked the sight once again.

Nice and easy. Squeeze the trigger, don't jerk it.

Inside No. 33 Banyard Road, Trevor Moore was standing motionless, staring at his captives.

Do it now.

Knott squeezed the trigger.

Nick Pearson ducked involuntarily as he heard the sharp retort of the HK81.

'They got tired of waiting,' he said, under his breath.

All along the street, uniformed and plain clothes policemen began running towards the house.

Moving at a speed in excess of two thousand feet a second, the 7.62mm bullet hit Trevor Moore in the left temple.

It tore easily through the temporal bone, ripped through the mass of grey matter inside then exploded from the other side of the skull leaving an exit wound the size of a fist.

Large gobbets of greyish-pink matter spattered the floor and wall, accompanied by several pulverised fragments of bone.

Moore remained upright for a second then pitched forward, blood spewing from the holes in his cranium.

★　　★　　★

Officer Lee Knott felt his stomach contract. He was going to vomit.

From inside the house, Nick Pearson heard screams.
  'Let's get to work,' he said.

8

Darworth, Hertfordshire, England

If the two black men knew they were being followed they gave no indication of it.

Raymond Carlton stayed ten or fifteen yards behind them all the way from the Work and Pensions building to the town centre, his gaze never leaving his quarry. When they slowed down, so did he. When they crossed streets he walked a few yards further up and did the same.

The centre of Darworth, like so many towns and cities, was pedestrianised, which was the reason Carlton had been forced to follow the two men on foot rather than remain in the Peugeot with his companions. Now he walked briskly along behind the two black men, narrowly avoiding a collision with a young woman who emerged from a clothes shop pushing a pram.

Carlton looked briefly at her. At the piercings in her left eyebrow and her lip. At the large tattoos on her exposed stomach and her right shoulder. The lank bottle-blonde hair that hung as far as her shoulders. She smiled at him and he returned the acknowledgement perfunctorily.

Ahead, the two black men had turned a corner. Carlton quickened his pace, pausing at the corner. He lit a cigarette, still watching the men as they continued on through a covered section of the shopping precinct. He saw them pause before a butcher's shop, glancing at the meat in the window for a moment before going in.

Carlton hurried past the shop and sat on one of the wooden benches opposite, his eyes on the black men inside the butcher's. They were obviously having trouble making themselves understood because he saw them pointing at several different cuts before the butcher finally found the meat they wanted.

Once they'd made their purchase, they walked out, heading towards the main road. Carlton got to his feet and followed.

As he left the pedestrianised centre and moved out into the main street he saw the large redbrick edifice of the council offices ahead of him and, on his left, the small three-screen cinema that served the town. Still oblivious of the fact they were being followed, the black men walked on.

There was a large park just beyond the council offices known locally as the rose gardens. Surrounded by poplars, it was an oval-shaped expanse of fountains, wooden benches, grass, gravel paths and rose bushes that had been designed to provide a pleasing and relaxing area for people to sit in. However, none of the fountains worked, the paths were overgrown, most of the benches had been broken or scarred with sharp instruments and Carlton couldn't ever remember seeing a rose bloom in there. The fact that a lot of the bushes had been either trampled down or dug up and stolen didn't help, he reasoned.

The two black men headed towards this barren space and wandered unconcernedly along one of the paths. Carlton decided to walk along the pavement that encircled the gardens. Every now and then he would glance through the poplars to ensure that he was level with the two men.

An old woman walking her pekinese crossed the road just ahead of him.

Because of him?

He glanced at her as he passed but most of his attention was on the two black men ahead of him. They had now crossed the park and were heading down a leafy road, away from the town centre.

Carlton stood where he was, pulled out his mobile phone and jabbed the digits he wanted.

He waited, glancing at the black men as they walked on.

I know where you're going.

'Yeah,' the voice at the other end of the phone said.

'Pick me up at the rose gardens,' Carlton snapped.

'Have you called him yet?' Paul Duggan asked on the other end of the line.

42

'I'm just going to,' Carlton informed his companion. 'Just get a move on.'

He ended the call then sucked in a deep breath and prepared to make the second, and more important, call.

As he jabbed the digits, he noticed that his hand was shaking slightly.

9

North Kensington, London, England

Nick Pearson nodded approvingly as he watched the monitor before him.

Seated on a large leather sofa in the editing suite, he drummed his fingers lightly on the arm. Next to him, Gordon Dale made a few hasty notes on the sheet of paper he held then glanced at Pearson.

At forty-two, Dale was four years older than his colleague. He was dressed in a beautifully tailored charcoal grey suit and his shoes gleamed as if they'd been cleaned with an industrial buffer.

Pearson couldn't have presented a more striking contrast. Clad in a black sweatshirt and faded jeans, he flicked at one of his trainer laces as he continued to gaze at the pictures in front of him.

After a moment or two he got to his feet, crossed to the water cooler on the far side of the suite and filled a paper cup. He dug in his jeans for a small bottle, took out a yellow tablet and swallowed it with a gulp of water.

'Headache?' Dale enquired as Pearson returned to sit beside him.

'No, they're Valium,' the younger man said. 'The doctor said they'd help. Only short term. Just until the business with my dad was over.' He massaged the bridge of his nose between his thumb and forefinger. 'Apparently they prescribe them quite regularly to the bereaved.'

'You should have taken more time off after your dad died. I told you that,' Dale reminded him.

'I appreciate that, Gordon, but I think getting back to work again quickly helped.'

'If it helped, why are you taking Valium?'

'It doesn't affect my ability to present the show, does it?'

'I didn't say it did. I'm concerned about *you*, Nick. Not the show.'

'Don't let the director general hear you say that.' Pearson smiled. 'Not concerned about the highest rated investigative news programme on TV?'

'You know what I mean.'

'So, let's talk about the programme instead of my private life, shall we?'

Dale shrugged. 'You still want to do this series, then?' he asked.

'Even more so after what happened in Bermondsey today,' Pearson told him.

'Trevor Moore was shot because he was a dangerous

crackhead holding a gun on his family. Not because he was black.'

'I know that. But do you think the police would have decided to take him out so quickly if he'd been white?'

'Yes.'

'You're probably right.'

'So how does that tie in with the programmes you want to make about the rise of racial violence in Britain over the last year? Moore was a drug addict. The police had no choice but to shoot him. If they hadn't he might have wiped out everyone else in that house.'

Pearson nodded. 'I know why they shot him, Gordon,' he said quietly.

The two men regarded each other silently for a moment then Pearson got to his feet again and crossed to a desk in front of the bank of monitors. He returned with an A4 clip file, which he opened.

'The number of racially motivated crimes in this country has risen by more than forty per cent during the last six months and that's both ways. Black against white and vice versa,' he said, flicking through the collection of news clippings inside the file.

'So why do you want to concentrate on one particular town? What's it called again?'

'Darworth. It's in Hertfordshire.'

'What makes it so special?'

'Because it's a small middle-England town,' Pearson told him. 'Not a big city with racial ghettos in it.

And there's no apparent reason for the explosion of racially motivated crimes there.' He got to his feet, suddenly enthused by what he was talking about. 'Fifteen arrests during the last two months. Racial attacks. A demonstration in the town centre against the African refugees living there that almost turned into a riot.' Pearson held up his hands in front of him. 'And all this in a predominantly middle-class English town.'

'I can understand why you want to do the programme, Nick,' Dale said slowly. 'I'm just wondering if there's not a better way of doing it. At least take a camera crew with you.'

'What could be better than me going to Darworth on my own and talking to the people there? Both sides. If I've got a crew with me I'll stick out like a sore thumb.'

'You will anyway. You won't be able to work undercover when people know who you are. They'll have seen you on TV. On this show, on the news.'

'That won't matter. People are sometimes more likely to speak to someone they think they know than to a complete stranger.'

'When do you want to leave?'

'Tomorrow. My hotel in Darworth's already booked.'

Dale shrugged. 'I'm not questioning your ability to do this, Nick. Just the wisdom of it,' the older man said. 'You're walking into a dangerous situation anyway but it's made more dangerous because—'

47

'Because I'm black?' Pearson interrupted. 'That's exactly what qualifies me best, Gordon.' He smiled. 'I want to collect information. Find out what's really happening in Darworth and why. When I've done that I'll go back with a crew and cover what I need to.'

Gordon Dale nodded slowly. 'If that's how you want to do it,' he said flatly.

'It is,' Pearson proclaimed. 'And that's how I *am* going to do it.'

Khasilah, twelve miles south of Tangier,
Northern Morocco

The tall man was woken by a sharp dig in his ribs. He sat bolt upright and looked in the direction of the truck driver, who was grinning at him.

'Time to get out,' the driver told him, swinging himself out of the cab and jumping down.

The tall man took a moment to recover his senses, peering around him through the dusty and cracked windscreen of the Scania at the landscape he now found himself in.

They seemed to be in a shallow valley. Hills sloped gently upwards to the east and west and the man could see a few meagre buildings clinging to the ridges. About five hundred yards from the dirt road where the lorry had stopped there was a train track. A siding, the rails rusted and the sleepers splintered, curved off from the main track. A battered and weather-beaten carriage stood alone on this offshoot, resting against some buffers.

The tall man waited a moment then clambered down from the cab. He walked slowly towards the back of the Scania, watching as his fellow travellers spilled out on to the dusty road. They stood forlornly beneath the blazing sun while the driver shouted at them to move more quickly. He pulled one or two of the stragglers from the back of the lorry then swung himself up on to the tailgate to check inside.

'Come on,' he yelled. 'Out.'

The two figures that remained in the truck didn't move.

The driver stepped into the reeking blackness and approached the first of the figures. It was a man in his forties. He was lying on his back with his arms at his sides.

'Get out, you lazy bastard,' the driver yelled, then kicked the man hard in the shin.

He didn't move.

The driver pressed two fingers hard against the man's throat, feeling for a pulse but not finding one. He dropped to one knee and swiftly went through the man's pockets but came up with only a few coins. He pocketed them and turned to the other figure, a woman in her twenties, slumped against one wall of the truck.

'End of the road,' the driver snapped, kicking her. 'Move your arse.'

The woman didn't stir.

The driver again felt for a pulse but, again, he

could find none. What he did see, however, was a St Christopher medal round her neck. He pulled it hard, snapping the chain, and pushed it into his pocket with the coins he'd taken from the man. Then, as the other Africans watched, he hooked his hands beneath the woman's armpits and dragged her to the end of the tailgate. With a grunt, he heaved her body out on to the road.

The tall man looked on impassively.

The driver hauled the other dead African out of the truck too then jumped down beside the two corpses.

'Go on, get away from here,' he said. 'All of you, go. This is as far as I take you.'

The tall man regarded him through his heavy-lidded eyes but didn't move.

'That means you too,' the driver said to him. 'Unless you want to pay me some more. If you do, I'll wait with you until the plane arrives.'

The tall man shook his head.

'If they don't come for you, what will you do?' the driver asked.

The tall man said nothing. He merely looked up into the cloudless sky.

Behind him, a train slowly rumbled past and some of the other Africans ran towards it. The tall man turned to watch as some of the fitter ones caught up and tried to pull themselves up on to its flat trucks. The others had already begun to wander off along the dirt road or towards the hills.

'Perhaps I should take some more of your money anyway,' the driver said. 'I did let you ride up front with me.' He took a step towards the tall man.

The speed of the movement was incredible.

The tall man pulled the knife free and held it close to the driver's throat. The tip of the serrated blade was almost touching the Moroccan's flesh. The man stepped back, his breath coming in gasps.

'All right,' he said, holding up his hands in surrender. 'Keep your money. But if they don't come, you're finished.'

The tall man glared at him but didn't move. He merely watched as the driver turned and hurried back towards the cab of the Scania.

Seconds later, exhaust fumes belched from the tailpipe and the truck pulled away, clouds of dust rising into the air around it.

The tall man watched the truck speeding off. He pushed the knife carefully back into his pocket then walked to the roadside, stepping over the body of the dead woman in the process. There were some skeletal trees close by. They didn't offer much shade but they would do for the time being.

The tall man sat down with his back against the trunk of one.

He watched the sky and waited.

10

Darworth, Hertfordshire, England

'I just want to know why.'

Paul Duggan downed what was left in his pint glass and shoved the empty receptacle across the table.

'We followed those black bastards, just like you told us to, and then, when we had them where we wanted them, you tell us not to touch them,' he continued, reaching for his cigarettes. 'I don't get it.'

Stephen Kirkland eyed the younger man unblinkingly and took a sip from his own glass. Two weeks short of his thirty-ninth birthday, he was a big, powerfully built man with close-cropped brown hair. On the left side of his neck a tattoo of a spider looked as if it was crawling towards his jaw. On his right forearm there was another design engraved on his skin, this time of a tiger.

He had eyes the colour of glowing sapphires.

The Red Squirrel was full to bursting. The

constant drone of chatter coupled with the neverending thump of music from the jukebox filled the air. Situated as it was in the town centre of Darworth, the pub was usually busy but on this particular evening it seemed to be even more densely populated than usual.

A man carrying two pints bumped against Kirkland as he passed.

'Sorry, mate,' the man said hastily as Kirkland shot him a vicious glance.

'Do you want sit on his fucking lap, you cunt?' Errol Lawler added as the man moved hurriedly away.

Kirkland watched as the man headed through the crowd to the open doors of the pub and out towards the area filled with metal tables and battered parasols. Then he slowly turned his attention back to Paul Duggan.

'It was broad daylight, you prick,' he said dismissively. 'I told you to follow them. I didn't tell you to sort them, did I?'

'So, when are we going to do something?' Duggan persisted.

'Soon,' Kirkland told him, finishing his own pint. 'Now stop moaning and get another round in.' He pushed his glass into the middle of the table. 'And get them to turn the volume down on that fucking jukebox while you're at it.'

Duggan hesitated a moment then got to his feet and walked reluctantly towards the bar, pushing and shoving his way through the throng of people.

'He's got a point, Steve,' Raymond Carlton said. 'I mean, spraying graffiti on walls is one thing but it's not going to make any of the black bastards move out, is it?'

'So what do you want to do?' Kirkland demanded. 'Hang one from a lamp post?'

Carlton grinned. 'It's an idea.'

'Yeah, well, believe me,' Kirkland said. 'If I had my way, I'd hang all the fuckers.' He turned in the direction of the jukebox as more music belted out.

Two girls in their early twenties were making a selection. Kirkland eyed them appraisingly, his gaze coming to rest on the shapely legs of the one who wore a short denim skirt.

She caught sight of Kirkland looking at her and said something to her companion. Both of them laughed before moving off in the direction of a table close to the bar.

'Slags,' Kirkland murmured under his breath.

Duggan returned and set down a tray of drinks on the table. He sat opposite Kirkland and swallowed some of his own beer.

'Are you working tonight, Steve?' Carlton asked.

'Not tonight,' Kirkland told him. 'I've got some time off.'

'I wish I had,' Duggan offered.

'You've got to have a job before you can have time off, you cunt,' Kirkland said.

The others round the table laughed.

'Yeah, and playing on an X-Box all day doesn't count,' Errol Lawler added.

'It sharpens your reflexes,' Duggan protested, downing more of his pint.

Lawler and Carlton laughed again.

'I put some flowers on Gary's grave today,' Kirkland said quietly. 'Tidied it up a bit, you know. That kind of thing.'

'See, that's another reason I don't understand why we're not doing something to these black bastards,' Duggan grunted. 'So, we give one of them a kicking every now and then. That's nothing. One of them killed your brother.'

'You don't have to remind me,' Kirkland rasped, glaring at him.

'I'd have thought you more than anybody would have wanted to do something,' Duggan continued, reaching out to take his glass again. 'Instead of just sitting around doing fuck all.'

Kirkland shot out one large hand and closed it round Duggan's, squeezing tightly.

'So what do you want me to do?' he hissed, holding Duggan's hand hard round the pint glass. 'I've got reasons for waiting and I don't have to fucking tell you, you little cunt.'

'I was just saying,' Duggan muttered, trying to pull his hand free but unable to break Kirkland's grip. 'I didn't mean anything by it, Steve.'

'Do you want me to kill one of them?' Kirkland asked, increasing the pressure so that Duggan could feel his own fingers and palm being forced ever more tightly against the glass.

'Do you want me to do it tonight?' Kirkland persisted.

'Steve, I'm sorry,' Duggan gasped, still unable to pull his hand away.

'You want blood?' Kirkland was leaning towards his younger companion now.

'Steve,' Carlton said, reaching out to touch Kirkland's arm.

'Keep out of this, Ray,' Kirkland snarled.

'He didn't mean anything,' Carlton insisted.

'He knows what he meant,' the blue-eyed man said. 'He's a big boy. He can talk for himself.'

'I just said—' Duggan protested, the pressure on his hand almost unbearable now.

'I know what you fucking said,' Kirkland interrupted through clenched teeth.

Even as the last word left his lips he tightened his grip more.

He heard the crack of breaking glass.

The tankard Duggan was holding shattered in his grip.

Two jagged pieces of it gouged into his palm, splitting the flesh. Blood and spilled beer washed across the tabletop in foamy reddish-brown streaks.

Duggan pulled his hand away as Kirkland released his vice-like hold.

'Fuck,' the younger man gasped, looking at the blood pumping from his gashed palm.

'Here,' Kirkland said dismissively, throwing his handkerchief at Duggan. 'Wrap that round it.' He looked down at the table. 'Waste of good beer. Good job you bought the fucking round.' He downed more of his own.

Duggan wound the piece of cloth quickly round his hand, seeing blood seeping through the material. When he looked across the table again he saw that Kirkland was still glaring at him.

'You want to do something?' the older man said, banging his empty glass down on the table. 'All right, then we'll fucking do something.'

11

St John's Wood, London, England

Nick Pearson rode the small lift to the second floor, gazing at his reflection in the mirrored walls.

As the lift bumped to a halt he stepped out, digging in his jacket pocket for his key. He let himself into his flat, closed the door behind him and stood with his back against the wood for a moment. He found the gloom inside the flat welcoming and passed from the hallway into the sitting room without switching on any lights.

The curtains were open so there was enough light from outside to prevent him from tripping over anything as he moved about. He switched on the television, the glow from the screen adding more illumination, and finally he clicked on a lamp that stood on a polished table.

He shrugged off his jacket and headed back out of the sitting room, walking down the carpeted corridor towards his kitchen, where he poured himself a glass of milk from the large fridge. There were some sausage rolls in there and Pearson took two. Taking a bite from one of them, he carried them and his milk back to the sitting room.

His laptop was on a table behind his sofa and he sat down before it and switched it on. He had a number of e-mails.

It was the third that really caught his attention. MOWENDE ON THE RUN.

Pearson frowned. He checked the e-mail, scanning the heading to see who had sent it, where from and at what time. It was from Donna Greeling, timed at 16:56.

'Donna,' Pearson murmured. He had known Donna Greeling for more than ten years. Worked with her on a number of occasions on various stories. He smiled as he thought of her. A tall, statuesque American with an infectious laugh who could drink most men under the table.

————

Dear Nick,

I thought you'd like to know that Victor Mowende has escaped. Check the agencies. I heard he left Sierra Leone two days ago. Disappeared into thin air. More info when I get it.

Love Donna.

————

Pearson sat back, still gazing at the screen.

'Mowende,' he muttered.

He tapped keys on the laptop and brought up several photos and articles, most of them authored by Pearson himself, charting the rise of Victor Mowende: an African politician who, until recently, had been imprisoned in Sierra Leone.

Pearson scanned the articles. The most recent had been written a year ago, and there was a photo next to it showing a mass grave filled with bodies. All had been machine-gunned by followers of Mowende.

Pearson had never forgotten finding the site. He, Donna Greeling and two other journalists had been travelling with some government troops when they'd made the grisly discovery. If he closed his eyes, he could still hear the cries of the wounded and the wailing of several children who had been standing around the open pit, one of them trying to pull his dead mother from the other corpses.

Pearson sat back from the screen, got to his feet and wandered across to the window. He gazed out into the street, sipping at his milk, and, despite the warmth in the room, he felt the hairs at the back of his neck rising.

'Mowende,' he muttered.

Madrid, Spain

The tall man stood close to the window of the fifth-floor apartment, looking down at the mass of vehicles speeding past on the Calle de las Huertas below.

Sometimes he would stand for what seemed like an eternity, gazing out at the traffic and the people. He was both amazed and repelled by the proliferation of both.

All his life he had seen people forced to live in close proximity to each other, crowded together like chickens on a battery farm. But this swarm of humanity seemed to excite different emotions within him. These people he watched were not his own. He looked on them contemptuously from his perch high above.

He had no desire to be in this place but he knew that he must endure it for another day or more, although the two men who had brought him here had assured him he would be taken onward soon.

The tall man was aware that there wasn't far to go now. The worst and most arduous part of his journey was over. His final destination beckoned.

What awaited him when he reached it he couldn't yet guess.

He hadn't left the apartment since his arrival two days earlier. Those who had brought him here had advised against it. Whatever he wanted they went out and fetched for him. They cooked for him, they bought him new clothes with the money he gave them. One of them had mentioned to him the possibility that he could have been followed. He would be wise not to leave the apartment. No one was to know of his whereabouts. It wasn't safe.

The tall man had tried to dismiss their concerns but he understood their anxiety, just as he understood their demeanour when they were around him.

For the most part they left him alone in the bedroom that was his. He watched the small television set they had installed for him, gazing at the images and listening to, but not understanding, the Spanish words spoken by the figures on the screen.

He ate in the living room or the kitchen of the apartment, always with one of the men close to him.

Watching.

And at these times he saw the look in the eyes of his guard.

It was fear.

The tall man had seen fear often enough in his life to recognise it when it coloured another's expression, and the knowledge that they were afraid of him pleased him. With fear came power.

That was something he knew only too well. It was a philosophy by which he'd lived most of his life.

Mixed with the fear there was reverence. They moved and spoke respectfully around him, and although he knew that the money they'd already been paid had helped to buy their allegiance, he knew too that they also continued to protect him because they were afraid of him.

That was why they brought him whatever he asked for.

Whatever he asked for.

The tall man stood by the window for a moment longer, then turned and headed across the sitting room towards his bedroom. The guard on the far side of the room watched him go and the tall man couldn't help but think that his companion felt relief. He moved through into his bedroom then on into the bathroom.

The room was small but well ventilated, for which he was grateful. The mutilated body that lay in the bath was beginning to decompose.

Soon the air would be thick with the stench of putrescence and not even the most sophisticated air conditioning would be able to mask the smell.

The eyes had already begun to turn to jelly, and as he stood over the small corpse the tall man could hear the soft hiss of gases from inside the body.

A sure sign that the internal organs were also beginning to rot.

The blood that had sprayed on to the walls had dried into thick brown smears.

A single bloated fly buzzed somnolently around the head of the corpse, occasionally settling on the ravaged features. It crawled over the parted lips and into the mouth, then disappeared up one of the nostrils for a second before continuing up one cheek.

The men who guarded him would clean the place up when he was gone. Just as they would dispose of the body.

The tall man looked down at it, his heavy-lidded eyes settling on the gaping hole in the chest where the heart had been torn out.

What remained of the heart now lay nearby on the edge of the sink.

There were still teeth marks in it.

12

Darworth, Hertfordshire, England

The three blocks of flats that dominated the Walden Hills estate looked like huge rotting teeth in the gloom.

Each of the blocks in Western Road was fifteen storeys high and contained sixty flats. The number of residents varied but it was generally estimated that each of the blocks held close to three hundred people.

When they'd been built, the flats had been state of the art: modern, well equipped and ideal for the families that had relocated to Darworth, mostly from major cities like London and Birmingham.

But those days, like the vast majority of the original tenants, were long gone.

The white-painted frontages of the buildings were dirty and badly in need of redecoration. Many of the windows that faced the street had been smashed. More were boarded up. The concrete walkways that connected the flats were littered with rubbish and stank of the urine and excrement of dogs and cats. Those lifts that worked also reeked of bodily waste, not all of it animal. The same was true of the battered concrete steps that offered the only certain access to the higher floors.

Outside each building there was a large tarmacked area for parking vehicles. Beyond that there was a grass verge, also littered with refuse and the faeces of pets.

Stephen Kirkland leaned against the side of the Peugeot and lit a cigarette, looking up at the flats with an expression of disgust on his face.

'Which ones?'

The voice behind him belonged to Raymond Carlton. Kirkland took a long drag on his cigarette and regarded the vehicles parked outside the flats.

'The van and that old Ford,' he said, nodding towards a dark blue, battered Transit and a silver–grey saloon.

Carlton nodded and moved to the back of the Peugeot. Kirkland heard the clang of metal on metal as his companion retrieved what he sought from the boot.

'Don't fuck it up,' Kirkland murmured, his eyes never leaving the tall buildings.

Carlton hesitated for a moment then scurried off, Errol Lawler running along beside him. They moved quickly and quietly in the darkness, invisible in the meagre glow cast by those few flats that had lights burning inside them.

Kirkland took another drag on his cigarette then dropped it into the gutter.

'Shall I start the engine?' Paul Duggan asked, his hand reaching for the Peugeot's ignition key.

'In a minute,' Kirkland said, still gazing at the flats.

He could barely see the outline of Carlton and Lawler as they moved among the motley selection of vehicles parked outside the flats. However, he smiled as he saw them pause beside the Transit. They made a few furtive movements then passed on to the rear of the car.

'Start the engine now,' Kirkland said, walking round to the passenger side.

Duggan did as instructed. 'Have they done it?' he asked.

Kirkland said nothing, but merely watched as Carlton and Lawler sprinted back towards the waiting Peugeot.

'What about this?' Carlton asked when they arrived, brandishing the empty petrol can in front of him as if it was some kind of trophy.

Kirkland pulled it from his grasp and threw it in the direction of the flats. Droplets of petrol sprayed out into the night air. The smell of the fuel was already strong in Kirkland's nostrils as he dug his hand in his jacket pocket and pulled out a box of matches.

He lit one, gazed at its flickering yellow flame for a second, then pushed it rapidly back into the box and dropped it on to the trail of petrol that Carlton and Lawler had left behind them.

The box went up with a small whoosh. The petrol caught fire immediately.

Kirkland pulled himself into the car, watching the flame trail speed across the grass verge then onwards over the tarmac towards the parked vehicles beyond.

'Go,' he snapped, flicking Duggan's arm.

The younger man stepped on the accelerator and the Peugeot shot away.

'You did what I told you, didn't you?' Kirkland asked, peering over his shoulder to the back seat. 'Put the rags in the petrol tanks?'

Carlton nodded.

Kirkland smiled as he saw the trail of fire reach the Transit. There was a loud explosion as the first vehicle went up. It was followed, moments later, by a second.

A shrieking plume of red and orange fire rose into the night air, a reeking black mushroom cloud of smoke spreading across the sky.

Kirkland turned to look at Duggan. 'Is that enough for now?' he mocked.

Duggan didn't speak.

Behind them, the flames leapt and danced madly as the vehicles were consumed.

13

The smell of burned flesh was strong in the air, an acrid stench that reminded Detective Sergeant Martin Bishop of charred meat. It mingled with the odour of petrol and the choking scent of burned rubber. A thin cloud of black smoke still wafted around the burned vehicles outside the flats in Western Road.

Bishop could see people on the balconies and walkways above him, all peering inquisitively down at the activity below, and the emergency vehicles with their blue lights turning silently in the dull light of the early morning. The DS looked at his watch.

Seven thirty-one a.m.

He glanced at a uniformed man who passed him carrying a piece of burned cloth secured in a transparent evidence bag.

'That was the fuse.'

The voice came from behind him and Bishop turned to see a slightly younger man approaching him. He had a shaven head and wore metal-rimmed glasses. Bishop could see small cinders sticking to one of his eyebrows.

'Not very subtle but effective,' Detective Constable Daniel Hall continued. 'A piece of old cloth screwed up, doused in petrol then stuck in the fuel tank and lit. Simple as that.'

'The arsonist lit it then legged it, right?' Bishop said.

'The Fire Brigade say they found petrol all round both vehicles, and the grass was burned all the way from where the car and van were parked back as far as the road.'

Bishop walked towards the burned-out van, running appraising eyes over the scorched chassis, occasionally waving his hand in front of his nose when the stench of seared rubber grew too intense. Then he moved to the rear of the vehicle and gazed at the contents.

The body that lay inside resembled a spent match.

As Bishop leaned closer he could see tiny wisps of grey smoke rising from the empty eye sockets and what remained of the nostrils. The teeth that hadn't been melted by the ferocity of the explosion and resulting fire gleamed brightly from the rictus of the charred features.

The fingers of the right hand had been burned down to the last knuckle, exposing the whiteness of the bone. It stood out in dazzling contrast to the incinerated flesh. The left hand was also badly burned, but not enough to disguise the mahogany colour of the skin.

'African?' Bishop mused, noting how dark the flesh was.

'Looks like it,' Hall said. 'We've got men interviewing the other occupants now, trying to find out if anyone knows who this guy is.'

'Did anyone inside the flats see what happened?'

'If they did they haven't said yet.'

'Someone must have seen or heard something,' Bishop insisted. 'Vans and cars don't blow up *quietly*, do they?' The DS waited a moment longer then stepped down from the rear of the van. He turned and headed back towards his car. Hall walked briskly along beside him.

'Do you think it's murder, guv?' the DC asked.

'Well, it doesn't look much like suicide, does it?' Bishop sighed.

'Terrible way to die. Burning.'

Bishop nodded. 'The only consolation is the poor bastard was probably killed by the explosion. Dead before he burned. We'll know more when we hear from the pathologist.'

'Who'd want to kill someone like that?'

'Christ knows,' Bishop conceded. 'I mean, if you want someone dead you stab them or shoot them. Chuck them off a building. You don't put them in the back of a Transit and blow the fucking thing up. It's too complicated. I don't think whoever torched that van knew that geezer was inside when they lit it up. I think we're looking for someone who fucked up. Pure and simple.'

14

Nick Pearson parked the Audi in the car park behind the George and Dragon Hotel, Darworth. He locked the vehicle and carried his small suit-case through the main entrance towards reception.

The drive from London had taken less than two hours and, using his satellite navigation, he'd found the George and Dragon with ease. It looked like a glorified Travelodge: a plastic hotel that boasted a restaurant and two bars, one of which contained a pool table. The carpet was in need of cleaning and so, Pearson noted, was the dark blue jacket of the thin-faced man behind reception.

He wore a gold name badge that identified him as Gareth.

'Room in the name of Pearson, please,' the reporter said, glancing around him.

Gareth nodded amiably and tapped Pearson's name

into the computer before him. He took Pearson's payment then handed him a plastic key card.

'Do you need any help with your luggage?' he asked perfunctorily.

'No thanks.'

'The lifts are to your right,' Gareth said, pointing with one bony finger.

Pearson smiled and made his way to the first floor where his room was. It was basic, but it looked comfortable enough.

15

Detective Sergeant Martin Bishop's office was on the second floor of the redbrick police station in Darworth.

From the large picture window behind his desk, he could see down into the car park of the building. His own car was parked there as well as several others, both marked and unmarked.

Beyond the car park lay the town's railway station. A tall metal fence, topped with razor wire, formed a boundary between the police car park and the sidings. There were several disused passenger carriages and some containers standing on the tracks.

The DS heard a goods train rumble through the station but the sound didn't disturb him. He reached for the coffee he'd just retrieved from the vending machine outside his office, wincing when he burned his fingertips on the thin plastic of the receptacle. He readjusted his grip and sipped at the hot liquid, his eyes scanning what lay on the desk before him.

Photographs of the burned-out Transit and car.

Close-ups of the dead man.

The fire officer's report.

Forensic observations.

Bishop blew out a weary breath, looking up almost gratefully when he heard a knock on his office door.

'Come in,' he called.

Detective Constable Daniel Hall entered. He was holding a manila file that he handed to his superior.

'Witness statements,' he announced. 'Most of the flats' residents don't speak very good English so I called in a translator to help.'

'Good lad.' Bishop grinned. 'Showing your initiative. Are you after my job?'

Hall grinned back. 'One day, guv,' he admitted.

Bishop opened the file and scanned the pieces of paper within.

'Nobody saw anything?' he muttered.

'No.'

'Any ID on the dead man yet?'

'Emmanuel Agassa,' Hall announced.

'Check it out with the council and the benefits office. See if they've got anyone registered under that name. If he was living in a council flat it must have been assigned to him and if he didn't have a job he was claiming benefit, so one or both of them might have some trace of him. And check the DVLA, see who the Transit and the car belonged to.'

Hall nodded.

'Forensics say the car and the van were both covered in prints,' Bishop added. 'Let's hope that the arsonist's prints are there too.'

'You mean the murderer's?'

Bishop shrugged.

'Do you reckon it's racially motivated?' Hall wanted to know.

'Two vehicles are torched outside the Western Road flats. Flats that are occupied exclusively by African refugees. The same flats that have been pelted with stones and sprayed with racist graffiti in the last few months. You don't have to be Sherlock Holmes to figure out the motive, Dan.'

'What did the pathologist's report say?'

'I haven't had it yet,' Bishop announced, getting to his feet. 'Let's go and find out.'

16

NIGGERS OUT

Pearson guessed that the bright red letters were at least six feet high.

As if they'd been daubed on using blood.

He pulled the digital camera from his pocket and took a couple of shots of the spray-painted wall. An old woman pulling a shopping trolley passed him and glanced curiously at him as he stood there with his camera. Pearson smiled thinly at her then continued on down the sloping walkway until he emerged into the central pedestrianised shopping precinct.

All the usual shops you'd expect to find, he noted as he walked; people going about their business alone or in small groups.

Nothing unusual here.

He saw a small café across the way and headed towards it, the smell of freshly cooked bread drawing him. He walked in and crossed to the counter where he ordered a sandwich and a pot of tea.

Carrying the plastic tray with his purchases balanced on it, he made for the rear of the café and seated himself with his back to the wall so that he could see who came and went.

Two girls in their teens were seated at one of the window tables comparing text messages. A man wearing paint-splashed overalls was reading a newspaper and sipping from a large mug of tea. A woman was struggling to feed her baby with a bottle while her older child spun round incessantly on the plastic-covered seat beside her.

Pearson chewed his sandwich and tried to blend in.

His mobile rang.

Muttering through a mouthful of sandwich he answered it, aware that several heads had turned in his direction.

'Hello,' he said, wiping crumbs from his mouth.

'Nick, it's me.' He recognised Gordon Dale's voice immediately. 'I just wanted to check you'd arrived all right.'

'I'm fine,' Pearson said. 'Just having a wander round. Is something wrong?'

'I don't know if you've seen or heard yet but they've had some more trouble there. One of the regional units reported it early this morning.'

'What kind of trouble?'

'An arson attack. A van and car were set on fire.'

'How do you know?'

'I'm in the news business like you, remember?'

'Racial?' Pearson asked, lowering his voice.

'I don't know. It happened at a place called the Western Road flats. It might be worth you checking it out.'

'Thanks for that, Gordon,' Pearson said. 'Speak to you later.'

17

Detective Sergeant Bishop guided the Astra into position close to an ambulance that had just pulled up outside the Accident and Emergency entrance of the Lister Hospital.

As he switched off his engine he glanced across at the vehicle and saw two paramedics helping a man out of the back into a wheelchair. The man was in his late fifties and his face was pale and greasy with sweat. He had a blanket round his shoulders, covering his pyjama jacket. His chest was bare and he was holding a plastic face mask over his nose, breathing deeply through it as he was wheeled through the automatic doors.

Bishop and DC Hall entered the building a few paces behind the stricken man. They showed their identification to the nurse behind the desk near the entrance, who merely nodded, more concerned with taking details from the two paramedics who'd pushed the wheelchair-bound occupant inside moments earlier.

Bishop glanced at the other patients waiting to be seen, then walked through a set of double doors and out into a long corridor which led to a lift. Bishop pressed the call button and the doors slid open almost immediately.

The detectives rode the lift to the basement where it bumped gently to a halt, the doors opening to release them. Bishop nodded in the direction of the sign that proclaimed MORGUE.

There were two empty gurneys outside the double doors leading into the morgue. Bishop wondered if the former occupants were now inside.

He pushed the doors open and walked in, followed by his colleague.

Apart from the steady dripping of a tap and the low buzz of the fluorescent lights in the ceiling, the place was silent. There were three stainless steel slabs in the room, the one furthest from them the only one occupied. Bishop moved slowly towards it, recognising the body on view.

'Where's George?' Hall wanted to know, peering round the room.

Bishop ignored the reference to the pathologist and stepped nearer to the burned body. He could see that the post-mortem had been carried out. The corpse had been opened up with the usual neck to groin incision, and the flaps of flesh had been pulled back to reveal the internal organs, some of which had already been removed. Bishop could see something deep red and gelatinous in the weighing scales above the dissection table. There were a number of scalpels, knives and saws lying on the metal trolley beside the slab, some stained with blood and other fluids.

The double doors leading into the morgue burst open and both men spun round.

George Hamblett was a stocky, powerfully built man in his mid-forties.

'We wondered where you were,' Hall said.

'Sorry to leave the place unattended,' Hamblett told them. 'Caught short.' He smiled. 'Even great men have to pee, you know.'

Bishop smiled. 'Thanks for sharing that with us, George. What do you make of our friend here?' He nodded towards the corpse.

'The victim was approximately thirty years old,' the pathologist announced, moving across to stand beside the two policemen. 'Unfortunately, the extent of the burning makes it difficult to give more precise answers. But look at this.'

He pointed to the left inner arm of the corpse.

Bishop leaned closer, noticing marks on the flesh that the older man was indicating.

There was a series of large Xs on the skin.

'Tattoos?' Bishop asked.

'No. It's scar tissue,' the pathologist informed him. 'There are more on the inside of the left thigh and also on the back of the neck at the base of the skull.'

'Could they be tribal marks of some kind?' Hall offered.

'It's possible,' Hamblett conceded. 'But they're relatively new. No more than a month or two. And that's why they're puzzling. My initial examination revealed that he'd already been dead for three months. Who'd want to carve crosses on a corpse?'

Bishop held up a hand to silence the pathologist.

'Hang on, George,' he said. 'What do you mean, he'd already been dead for three months?'

'That man didn't die last night. The blast didn't kill him and neither did the fire.'

'So what did?' Bishop wanted to know.

'It's hard to say at the moment.'

'So why do you think he was killed before last night?'

'You can tell by the exterior condition of the body,' the pathologist explained. 'At least the areas of skin not so badly burned.' He used the tip of the scalpel as a pointer, aiming first at the head and then at the groin of the dead man. 'The face is swollen. So is the scrotum. And there's blistering of the skin on the buttocks and several other places.'

'Couldn't that have been caused by the fire?' Bishop asked.

Hamblett rubbed the scalpel blade gently over an area of flesh at the top of the dead man's right hip.

'Burned flesh would have calcified. Hardened,' he said. 'The skin here is still relatively supple.' He continued moving the scalpel back and forth and

Bishop watched as several layers of almost liquescent flesh peeled away. It reminded the detective of wet toilet tissue.

'So, was he murdered or not?' the DS asked. 'If not last night then three months ago?'

'He wasn't poisoned,' Hamblett said. 'I've already tested the contents of the stomach, the blood and the urine. There don't appear to be any gunshot or knife wounds anywhere on the body either.'

'Strangulation?' Bishop offered.

'It's possible,' the pathologist said, nodding. 'The larynx was destroyed by the fire and so were the eyes. That makes it difficult to determine whether he was killed that way.'

'So, if there hadn't been an arson attack last night, his body might still be in that van?' Bishop murmured.

'Maybe the killer wanted it to look like an arson attack to cover up the murder,' Hall suggested.

'Then why leave him in there for three months?' Bishop retorted. 'Why not just burn the corpse as soon as they murdered him? They could still have used the same story.'

The three men stood silently round the body, gazing down at it.

'What the fuck is going on?' Bishop said.

18

There were blue and white plastic strips of tape bearing the legend POLICE – DO NOT CROSS set up round the skeletal remains of the burned-out vehicles.

Nick Pearson slid the digital camera from his jacket pocket and took several shots before clambering out of the Audi and wandering across the wide road in the direction of the Western Road flats, gazing up at the three huge monolithic towers as he did so.

He glanced around and saw that several people, mostly children, were peering at the remains of the Transit and the car. Some of them looked in Pearson's direction as he approached.

He smiled amiably and moved closer to the blue and white cordon.

'Did you see what happened here?' he asked a black teenage boy.

The boy looked at Pearson appraisingly then shook his head.

'Are you a policeman?' a younger boy asked.

'No.'

'Then why are you here?' another voice asked.

It belonged to a woman. She was tall and willowy, her jet black hair pulled back so hard it seemed to have stretched the skin of her forehead.

'I heard there'd been some trouble,' Pearson told her. 'I wanted to see for myself. Was anyone hurt?'

The woman shrugged.

'Which part of Africa are you from?' Pearson enquired.

The woman looked shocked.

'I recognise your accent,' he explained.

'You are not African,' she challenged him.

'No, but I've spent a lot of time there. Working. I'm a journalist. A reporter.'

'What will you say about this?' she asked, nodding in the direction of the burned-out vehicles. 'Will you tell the truth?'

'What is the truth?'

'That white men did this because they hate us. Because they want us to move away from here.'

'Do you know it was white men?'

'It's always white men.' She sneered. 'The same ones who throw stones. Who spit at us. Who paint insults on walls.' She looked him up and down. 'They would kill us if they could get away with it.'

'Don't the police do anything to help you?'

'White police aren't interested in helping Africans,' she snapped.

'What else has happened in this town?'

'People have been attacked. Beaten,' she said. 'They treat us like animals. We did not ask to come here. All we want is to live in peace but they will not let us.'

'How long have you been here?'

'A year. I came here with my daughter. We escaped from one kind of fear only to find another.'

'Where did you come from?'

'Sierra Leone.'

'Is that where the other people who live here are from?'

'They are from all over Africa.'

'What's your name?' he asked gently.

'Emily Juma,' she said reluctantly.

'My name is Nick Pearson,' he told her, fishing in his pocket. He pulled out a business card and offered it to her. 'Take this. If you want to speak to me it's got my phone number on it.'

'If I do, will you tell the truth?' she demanded, turning away from him.

Pearson could only nod.

He watched her as she walked away.

19

The cellophane wrapping round the flowers crackled as Stephen Kirkland laid the blooms on the grass below his brother's marble headstone, reaching out to trace the name engraved on the stone with one index finger.

A gentle breeze blew across Copsley Fields, bringing with it the scent of flowers from other graves. There were a lot of them: it was Darworth's largest cemetery. Kirkland removed the dead and dying stems he himself had arranged in the metal vase on his last visit, replacing them with the fresh flowers he'd purchased that morning.

As he knelt beside the grave he glanced around him and saw that there were three other visitors to the vast necropolis. They were tending graves too, one of them busily cleaning a headstone with a cloth and talking softly as she worked, Kirkland presumed to the occupant of the resting place.

He smiled to himself. 'I wonder if they can hear?' he murmured, continuing with his own ministrations. Using a tissue, he wiped the plinth that the vase stood on. 'Can you hear me, Gary? I hope so. I hope you can see me too.'

He pushed more flowers into the vase, threading them into the holes in the top of the receptacle. 'What I did last night I did for you,' Kirkland continued. 'Everything I do is for you. I call it justice. Because you never got any, did you? All this time and they still don't know who murdered you. Don't know and don't fucking care.' He pushed another flower in among the others. 'I'd change places with you like that.' He snapped his fingers. 'It shouldn't have been you.' He sucked in a deep breath. 'But I promised myself when it happened that I'd never let it go. Some fucker's going to pay for what happened to you. I swore that then and I swear it again.' He pressed his hand to the cold marble of the headstone.

Another breeze blew gently across the cemetery and Kirkland momentarily closed his eyes.

'Is that you telling me you can hear me, Gary?' he whispered. 'I know you'd have done the same for me. Never let it rest until someone had paid.'

He heard footsteps behind him, crunching on the gravel pathway that cut through the graveyard from one side to the other.

Kirkland turned to see an old man making his way towards one of the litter bins dotted around the cemetery. He was moving slowly, almost painfully, with the aid of a walking stick. He nodded a greeting as he passed and Kirkland returned the gesture before turning back to face the headstone.

'The others don't really understand,' he continued, screwing the dead flowers up in the cellophane. 'How could they? They're only kids. They've never lost anyone close to them. Not yet. When it happens they'll know what this feels like. They'll know what a great big fucking hole it leaves inside when somebody you love dies.' He got to his feet. 'I felt it when our mum died, but not as bad as this. At least she was old. She'd had a good life. Not like you. Twenty-eight. You should have had another forty or fifty years.'

He stepped back a couple of paces, running his eyes over the marble headstone, satisfied that it was sufficiently clean. However, he did notice some weeds growing on the grave near the plinth. He ducked down and pulled them free, pushing them into the crumpled cellophane with the dead flowers.

'I'll see you again soon, Gary,' he said quietly, then turned and headed for the path.

As he approached the dustbin near the main gates, Kirkland saw that the old man with the walking stick was now seated on one of the wooden benches nearby. He stuffed the cellophane parcel and the dirty tissue into the bin and, once more, the old man nodded agreeably in his direction.

'You all right, mate?' Kirkland asked, noticing that the old man was breathing heavily.

'Yes, thanks, son,' the man told him, patting his chest. 'Not so easy to get around at my age, that's all.'

'I've seen you here before.'

'I come every day to see my wife. What about you? If you don't mind me being nosy. Who are you visiting?'

'It's my brother.'

'I'm sorry.'

'Yeah, so am I.' Kirkland wiped some dirt from his hands and turned to leave.

'They're in a better place,' the old man offered.

Kirkland nodded. 'I hope you're right, mate,' he said.

The old man put his hand to his chest and took another deep breath.

'Are you sure you're OK?' Kirkland asked again.

'Just short of breath. It's kind of you to ask. Thank you. I'll sit here for a bit. I'll be fine.'

'You take care of yourself.'

The old man smiled warmly.

Kirkland walked briskly away in the direction of his car. As he slid behind the wheel he took one last look at the old man. He was still seated on the bench, leaning forward slightly on his stick.

Kirkland started his engine.

As he did so, the first spots of rain dotted the windscreen.

20

From where he was now parked, Nick Pearson had a clear view of the main entrance to Darworth police station.

He took a drag on his cigarette and watched as another police car pulled up before the building. Two uniformed men got out, one of them moving to open the rear passenger door.

The two men who emerged from the back seat were both tall, lean-looking black men who looked at the policemen with a mixture of bewilderment and anxiety on their faces.

Pearson reached for his camera and took a picture. It joined the dozen or so he'd already taken in the last thirty minutes.

A steady procession of marked and unmarked cars had pulled up outside the police station, each of them with at least two passengers. Always black. Like the people he'd seen at the Western Road flats earlier that day.

Pearson had seen the men enter the building, escorted by constables or plain clothes officers. One or two of the Africans had worn amiable expressions, but for the most part the individuals he had photographed had appeared nervous, fearful or, in two or three cases, suspicious or wary.

None of those who had entered, Pearson noted, had yet left. He wondered if they were being held pending further investigation.

He took another picture of the two newest arrivals as they were shepherded through the main entrance, one of them pausing just in front of the doors. Pearson could see the man's lips moving as he spoke to the constable nearest to him but the uniformed man merely nodded and put a firm hand on the African's shoulder, guiding him into the building.

Pearson took another drag on his cigarette and massaged the back of his neck with one hand. He scrolled through the photos he'd already taken, inspecting each of the Africans' faces.

The police obviously suspect that the vehicles were torched by one of the people living inside the flats. The residents are in no doubt that it's a racially motivated crime.

He sucked in a deep breath.

Are the police trying to shift the blame or have they already found the culprit? Is he inside now, sitting in a cell?

There was a story here. No doubt about it. Something major.

'Racial warfare in middle England,' he murmured to himself.

Emily Juma had no doubt it was racially motivated, did she? What about the other Africans who lived there? Go back, talk to some more of them. Ask their opinions. Find some of the ones who have been questioned here today.

Pearson caught sight of his reflection in the rear-view mirror. He yawned and stretched, wondering if he might be better served going back to his hotel and having a few hours' rest. The sleep he couldn't enjoy at night, he thought, he might at least be able to make up for now. He had never been able to sleep in hotels.

Take a couple of Valium tonight before you go to bed. They'll help.

He finished his cigarette and dropped the butt out of the window. Then he shook himself and took a couple of deep breaths. Swinging himself out of the Audi, he locked it and strode towards the main entrance of Darworth police station.

21

As the door of his office opened, Detective Sergeant Martin Bishop looked up to see a uniformed sergeant standing there.

'What is it, Frank?'

'This gentleman asked if he could see you, sir,' the sergeant said. 'He says it's important.'

He stepped aside and ushered Nick Pearson forward.

Bishop held the newcomer's gaze for a moment, then nodded.

'Thanks, Frank,' he said to the sergeant, who left, closing the door behind him.

'Detective Sergeant Bishop,' Pearson said cheerily, stepping further into the room. 'Good to meet you.'

'I know you,' Bishop said. 'You're on TV. I've seen you.'

'Nick Pearson,' the newsman said, extending his right hand.

Bishop hesitated a moment then shook it perfunctorily.

'We're pretty busy at the moment, Mr Pearson,' he said.

'Yes, I know. The arson investigation.'

'How do you know about it?'

'I'm a newsman.' Pearson smiled. 'It's my business to know.'

'You haven't come to a place like Darworth to investigate an arson attack,' Bishop said. 'Why are you really here?'

'I won't lie to you. I'm working on a series of programmes about the rise of racial violence in this country and, as you'll know better than anyone, the increase in Darworth seems to be disproportionately large considering the kind of town Darworth is.'

'And exactly what kind of town *is* Darworth, Mr Pearson?'

'Well, it's not the kind of place you'd expect race riots, is it?'

'We haven't had riots here.'

'But you have had a disproportionately large rise in racial crimes over the last few months, haven't you?'

Bishop merely regarded his visitor evenly.

'This arson attack is racially motivated, isn't it?' Pearson went on. 'The Africans who live at the Western Road flats seem to think so.'

'It looks as if it could be,' Bishop said reluctantly.

'Any suspects yet?'

'We're interviewing the residents of the Western Road flats. We need to know if anyone can tell us anything about the man who died in the burned-out van.'

'So it's a murder investigation?'

'We found a body, yes.'

'Do you know who he is?'

'His name's Emmanuel Agassa. He was an African refugee. More than likely illegal like a lot of them. Other than that, we've got nothing so far. That's why we're interviewing the other residents.'

'Do you think one of them killed him?'

'It's possible.'

'Isn't it possible he was killed by racists?'

'That's possible too.'

'Which part of Africa did he come from?'

'We don't know that yet.'

'What about the other residents of those flats? Where do they come from?'

'Ghana, the Congo, Guinea. All over. There are Nigerians, Senegalese and Christ knows what else living there. Probably from every country in Africa.'

'The woman I spoke to was from Sierra Leone.'

'Well, you were lucky she spoke to you. A lot of them can't or won't speak to us.'

'Perhaps they don't trust you. After all, the police haven't got a great record when it comes to dealing with ethnic minorities, have they?'

'Look, Mr Pearson, I'm very busy. I can't really

help you and to be honest, I'm not sure I want to. I know the type of programmes you do. I saw the one about institutionalised racism in the police force. That's obviously what you're really interested in.'

'I might be able to help you, Detective.'

'Can you speak any African languages?'

'I was born in Stepney,' Pearson confessed.

Bishop smiled in spite of himself. 'Listen, Mr Pearson—' he began.

'Nick,' the newsman interrupted.

'This inquiry would be conducted in the same way if it had been a white guy we'd found,' Bishop said.

'You don't have to justify yourself to me, Detective.'

'I'm not,' Bishop snapped. 'I just don't want the bleeding heart liberals sticking their noses in and crying that this investigation is an example of police racism. It makes no difference if the victim was white, Chinese, Russian, Brazilian or Asian. Somebody's dead and my job is to find the killer.'

'Like I said, I might be able to help you,' Pearson persisted. 'I've worked in Africa a lot.'

'Doing what?'

'I was a political correspondent for the BBC and for Reuters for nine years before I came back home.'

'I'll bear that in mind,' Bishop told him un-enthusiastically. 'Where are you staying?'

'At the George and Dragon Hotel.'

Bishop nodded. The phone on his desk rang and he picked it up.

'Bishop,' he said. He covered the mouthpiece quickly with one hand and looked at Pearson. 'I'm going to have to ask you to leave, Mr Pearson.'

The newsman nodded and got to his feet. When the door had closed behind him, the DS returned to his caller.

'Dan. Is there a problem?'

'The body we found in that van,' Daniel Hall told him. 'It's disappeared from the hospital morgue.'

22

As Detective Sergeant Martin Bishop stepped out of the lift that had carried him to the basement of the Lister Hospital he saw a uniformed policeman standing in the corridor.

'Where's DC Hall?' he asked.

'Inside the morgue, sir,' the constable answered.

Bishop strode on, and pushed the double doors open. He stepped inside the room, glancing around him as he did so.

Detective Constable Daniel Hall turned to greet his superior.

'Who reported the body missing?' Bishop asked.

'One of the morgue attendants,' Hall informed him. 'There are two. They each work twelve-hour shifts. One's already given a statement. They've both got cast-iron alibis.'

'Have the print boys been over everything?'

Hall nodded. 'There should be a report on your desk by four this afternoon.'

'So someone took him from the slab, did they?' Bishop murmured, walking to the stainless steel table where the body of the dead man had lain the previous night.

'No. After George finished the post-mortem he said he stood and watched while the morgue attendant put the body into one of the lockers.' Hall nodded towards the banks of metal storage compartments.

'The post-mortem was finished, then? The body had been sewn back up?'

Bishop walked across to the lockers. He could see the shiny carbon powder that had been brushed over the outside of the one that had contained the corpse. Several fingerprints were visible.

'Do we know who these belong to yet?' Bishop asked, indicating the prints.

'The two morgue attendants, the pathologist and a couple of doctors who work here at the hospital,' Hall told him.

'None of whom would have a reason to remove the body.'

'Who *would* have wanted to take it?'

'If I knew that, Dan, I'd be out arresting them now, wouldn't I?' Bishop moved back slightly, looking from the locker to the dissection table then at the tiled floor beneath. 'Did anyone see or hear anything? Whoever took the body would have had to carry it out of the hospital or wheel it out on a gurney or something.'

'And they'd have had to take it up the stairs or use the lift to get it out. They're the only two ways out of the basement.'

'No witnesses?'

'Not so far.'

'Someone must have seen something.'

'Well, if they did they haven't said so yet, guv.'

'These are locked, aren't they?' Bishop pointed to the metal cabinets before him. 'Who's got keys?'

'The morgue attendants. That's it. There's a spare set in their office. They've been dusted for prints but theirs are the only ones on there.'

'So when George finished the post-mortem, the body was put into one of the compartments, which, as far as we know, was then locked. No one sees anybody enter or leave the morgue during that time and not a soul sees a dead body being carried or wheeled out of here. That's about the size of it, right?'

Hall nodded.

'Last night we had a racially motivated arson attack on our hands.' Bishop sighed. 'Now, not only have we got a possible murder case to sort out, we've got a fucking body snatcher to deal with.'

23

Some of them knew of him.

Most had heard his name before.

A handful had even met him.

Many wondered why he was here. Now. Among them in this place so far from their homeland. The place that they would call theirs for the foreseeable future. This environment they now chose to call home.

The majority of those who lived in the Western Road flats on the Walden Hills estate in Darworth knew they could never return to the towns and villages where they had been born and raised. It was something they had resigned themselves to when they fled.

None of them had found life in this new country easy. They had struggled with the language and with some of the people whose land they now shared. They knew they were not wanted. Not popular. But the fear in which many lived was infinitely prefer-able to the circumstances in which they had existed before.

There were few among them who had not lost family members to the ravages of civil war, govern-mental oppression, starvation or genocide. None of these faced them in this new land. For the most part, they lived peacefully here.

Then he came.

Came from the country so many had called home. Arrived unexpectedly to live among them. And, for some, the fear that they had forgotten resurfaced.

Those who knew of him were afraid because they didn't know the extent of his power.

Those who knew his name feared him because of the stories they'd been told.

And those who had met him before felt as if they had stepped back into a nightmare from which they thought they'd escaped.

But they welcomed him into their midst. Like chickens welcoming a fox. They accepted him as one of their brothers because they hadn't the courage to do otherwise. Even though they were many and he was one. And, when he spoke, they listened. Mostly for fear of what might become of them if they didn't.

They had seen what he could do, this tall man with the heavy-lidded eyes.

The man who had come to them by plane, boat and train.

He had reached this place the same way as they had but they were sure his reasons for being here were as different from theirs as night from day.

They had sought refuge.

They had wanted only to live in peace and safety.

What he wanted among them, none could guess. Few tried to.

They knew that they would learn the reason eventually but, for the time being, many felt that his purpose was best left undiscovered.

24

Detective Sergeant Martin Bishop read the report again, shaking his head gently in the process.

Just as he had done the previous three times he'd read it.

He finally dropped the A4 sheets on to his desk and sat back in his chair running both hands through his hair.

It doesn't make sense. However you look at it. It doesn't make sense.

The DS got to his feet and crossed to his office window, where he stood gazing out across the car park towards the train station beyond. A passenger train had just pulled up and was disgorging its cargo of travellers. Bishop watched as they made their way towards the footbridge that led to the station exit.

He was still gazing at the tableau when there was a knock on his office door.

'Yeah,' he called, turning to see DC Hall entering

the room. The younger man was carrying two plastic cups, one of which he set down on the desk before Bishop.

'I thought you might want a coffee, guv,' he said.

'Cheers, Dan.' Bishop smiled. 'Something stronger might be more welcome at the moment.' Both men sat. 'So, what did we get from the Africans? Anybody with a motive for killing Emmanuel Agassa?'

Hall shook his head. 'Nothing so far, guv,' he said, almost apologetically. 'We've taken over a hundred statements here and up at the flats but we've still got nothing useful.'

'What *have* we got?' Bishop took a sip of his coffee.

'The Transit was registered in the name of Samuel Macanga. He lives at the Western Road flats. He bought the van second hand about a year ago. All the documents are in order.'

'Did he know Agassa?'

'Seen him around but didn't know him.'

'So he's got no idea how Agassa came to be dead in the back of his van?'

'If he has he's not saying.'

'What do you think, Dan?'

'Gut instinct? He had nothing to do with Agassa. He seemed more pissed off that his van had been torched. He works in a restaurant in town washing dishes. He used the van to drive there, and he's going to have to walk to work now.'

Bishop nodded. 'So, no motive and now no corpse,' he murmured.

'What did forensics turn up?'

'I've just been reading the report,' said Bishop, tapping the paper before him on his desk. 'It seems the more details we get, the more complicated this case becomes.' He exhaled deeply. 'All the prints you'd expect to find were in the morgue. Pathologist, doctors, morgue attendants and some nurses. Nothing unusual. Except for one set.'

Hall looked more intently at his superior.

'A set of Agassa's prints were found on the inside of the morgue doors,' Bishop said. 'The *inside.*'

'I'm not with you, guv.'

'He was dead when he was taken in there, Dan. How the fuck did his prints get on the inside of the doors? They open outwards. You have to push them from the inside to open them.' Bishop reached for the report and scanned it. '"Other matter found on inside of morgue door,"' he read aloud. '"Fragments of the same matter also discovered on floor of morgue, in corridor outside and on stairs leading from basement."'

'What kind of matter?'

'Burned human flesh,' Bishop said heavily. He dropped the report back on to his desk. 'Agassa's flesh. When his body was stolen I can understand that fragments of his skin might have flaked off and dropped on to the floor in the morgue and outside in the corridor. But you tell me how the fuck it got on the stairs leading up from the basement.'

'The body snatcher carried the corpse out?'

'Instead of using a trolley to move it? Instead of wheeling it into the lift then travelling up to the ground floor and just pushing it out of the hospital? Doesn't make much sense, does it, Dan?'

Hall could only manage a shrug as he looked at his superior.

'It gets better,' Bishop told him, smiling grimly. 'According to this forensic report, there were footprints found on the morgue floor, in the corridor outside and on the stairs leading up from the basement. Those footprints exactly match those of Emmanuel Agassa. If we believe what's in here,' Bishop tapped the report once more, 'no one stole Agassa's body from the morgue of the Lister Hospital. It got up by itself and walked out.'

25

Nick Pearson heard a satisfyingly loud crack as he slammed the cue ball hard into the pack.

Pool balls shot across the table in all directions.

Several of the other occupants of the George and Dragon's bar looked round as the sound reverberated throughout the room. Pearson spun the cue theatrically in one hand then walked round the table, picking his next shot.

He ducked down, selected a colour and slammed it into a middle pocket. As he straightened up he reached for the small cube of blue chalk and rubbed it across the rubber tip of the cue. When he hit the cue ball again a small cloud of the blue particles floated up from the point of impact.

He was selecting his next shot when he saw the main doors of the bar swing open.

The two young men who walked in, Pearson guessed, were in their early twenties. The first was wearing a black baseball cap over his short blond hair. The other ran appraising eyes over Pearson then dug in the pocket of his baggy jeans and pulled out a ten pound note. They crossed to the bar and Pearson heard them order drinks.

As they walked towards the seating area near the pool table, the one in the baseball cap slapped a coin on to the wooden lip of the baize.

'We're playing next,' he said, brushing past Pearson without looking at him.

The journalist glanced indifferently at the two newcomers as they sat down at the table next to the one where he'd put his own jacket.

Arrogant little prick.

'Unless you want a game,' Baggy Jeans called, sipping at his pint.

'No thanks,' Pearson told him. 'I don't mind playing on my own.'

'Oh, right,' Baseball Cap grunted. 'Rather play with yourself, would you?' He and his companion laughed. 'Play with yourself then,' Baseball Cap repeated.

'Very funny,' Pearson said under his breath.

Fucking dickhead.

'What?' Baseball Cap called.

Pearson lined up his next shot.

'You said something,' snapped Baseball Cap, wiping his mouth with the back of his hand.

Pearson shrugged. 'Not to you,' he answered, driving the ball towards one of the top pockets. It struck the jaws and spun out.

'You missed the hole,' Baseball Cap observed.

'Put some hair round it next time,' Baggy Jeans added and, once more, both of them laughed.

Pearson shook his head and took another shot.

'Got it,' Baggy Jeans noted.

'About time,' his companion added.

'Look, lads, if I wanted a commentary I'd hire the BBC, all right?' Pearson said, walking round the table. 'I just want to finish the game. And the quicker I finish the quicker you two get to play.'

'Fuck off,' Baseball Cap snorted indignantly.

Pearson glanced at the two younger men.

I wonder what you'd look like with a pool cue shoved up your arse, you mouthy little twats?

He saw one of them look across at his jacket then nudge his companion.

They must have seen the digital camera.

Pearson took another shot and missed, his attention now drawn towards the young men and the interest they were showing in his jacket. He gripped the cue in one hand and walked the two strides across to the table where his drink was perched. He took a sip of it.

'Get a move on, will you?' Baseball Cap said, looking at him disdainfully.

'Listen, mate, I don't want any trouble,' Pearson said.

'I ain't your fucking mate, right?' sneered Baseball Cap.

'Why don't you just go now?' Baggy Jeans suggested. 'Finish your drink and go.'

115

'Yeah, just fuck off,' Baseball Cap added venomously.

Pearson downed what was left in his glass and returned to the table, where he potted two more balls.

Baseball Cap had moved closer to Pearson's jacket and was glancing down at it.

What do you do? Lay one out with the cue, grab your jacket and run for the car?

Pearson took another shot and missed.

Don't start anything. If they have a go then defend yourself, but otherwise, forget it. Just get out. Do the sensible thing for a change.

One more ball left.

Pearson bent low over the table, lining up his shot, his gaze occasionally flickering in the direction of the two young men.

He saw Baseball Cap reach towards his jacket, his hand closing round the object Pearson knew to be his digital camera.

'Leave that alone,' he said, straightening up.

'Fuck off,' Baseball Cap grunted, holding the camera. 'You want it back, you come and fucking get it.'

Pearson looked from one to the other, trying to remain as calm as he could.

'All right,' he said finally, dropping his cue on to the pool table. 'You win. I've finished. Play your game. Just put the camera down.'

'Bollocks,' Baseball Cap snapped, turning it in his

hand. 'What kind of pictures have you got on here then? Some of your girlfriend?'

'Put the camera down,' Pearson insisted, taking a step towards the two younger men.

'Shall we have a look?' Baseball Cap said, grinning at his companion. 'I reckon he's got dirty pictures on here. That's why he doesn't want us to see them. I bet there's some of his girlfriend with her fucking ankles behind her ears.'

'Put the camera down,' Pearson said, his anger beginning to overcome his fear of what might happen. He moved closer to the table where the younger men sat.

The other occupants of the bar turned to watch. Pearson could feel his heart thudding hard against his ribs.

He turned quickly and saw that the barmaid was also watching.

'I'll get her to call the police,' he said, hooking a thumb over his shoulder.

'Go on then,' Baseball Cap said defiantly, still holding the camera.

Pearson could feel the knot of muscles at the side of his jaw throbbing angrily.

Drop the little bastard. Pick up the pool cue and whack him with it.

The journalist glanced quickly back towards the table, wondering whether or not to reach for a weapon.

Come on. You've been in more dangerous situations

than this in your life. Do something. They're fucking kids and they're making you look like a clown.

Pearson reached for the cue and hefted it before him.

'I'm going to ask once more,' he said quietly, glaring at Baseball Cap.

The younger man slammed his pint down on to the table and got to his feet, still holding the camera.

'Come on then,' he hissed.

26

'Just sit down and stop acting like a cunt.'

The voice boomed across the bar like a gunshot resounding over deserted woodland. Pearson turned in the direction of the shout.

Stephen Kirkland strode towards Baseball Cap, a look of irritation on his face.

'You heard,' he rasped. 'Now give him the fucking camera back.'

Pearson stepped back as Kirkland swept past him, hand outstretched. Baseball Cap dropped the digital camera into Kirkland's palm and sat down.

'Yours, I think,' Kirkland said, passing the Nikon to Pearson.

'Thanks,' Pearson murmured, still puzzled by what was happening.

'What the fuck are you doing, Steve?' Baggy Jeans gaped, similarly baffled by Kirkland's behaviour.

'Don't you recognise him?' Kirkland said, gesturing

towards Pearson. 'He's on the fucking TV. A big star. Important man.'

'But he's a nigger,' Baggy Jeans protested.

'I'll leave you to it,' Pearson offered, reaching for his jacket.

'No, don't run off,' Kirkland said. 'Stay and have a drink. You do drink with white blokes, don't you?'

Pearson regarded the tattooed man warily.

'Go on,' Kirkland persisted. 'These two cunts can buy it. It's the least they can do after messing you about like that.'

'There's no way I'm buying a drink for a nigger,' Baseball Cap muttered.

'Do as I tell you,' Kirkland snarled.

Pearson regarded the two younger men guardedly, not sure whether he really wanted to spend any more time in their company than was necessary.

'Just one,' Kirkland insisted.

Pearson nodded and sat down, aware that he was still holding the pool cue.

'What were you going to do with that?' Kirkland laughed, taking it from him.

'I'm not really sure,' Pearson admitted.

'This is Nick Pearson off the telly,' Kirkland told the two younger men. 'He's a news reporter.' He nodded towards Baseball Cap. 'This is Paul Duggan. This one,' he pointed at Baggy Jeans, 'is Ray Carlton.'

Neither of the younger men spoke.

'Get the fucking drinks in then,' Kirkland snapped. 'I'll have the usual. Nick, what are you having? You don't mind if I call you Nick, do you?'

Pearson shook his head. 'Just a mineral water,' he said.

'Go on then.' Kirkland pointed towards the bar, and the two younger men ambled away somewhat reluctantly.

'Sorry about that,' Kirkland said, watching them go. 'They're good lads really.'

'I'll take your word for that,' Pearson murmured. 'Are they that welcoming to all strangers or just to black ones?'

'Black faces aren't usually welcome in here, Nick,' Kirkland announced. 'By the way, my name's Stephen Kirkland.' He extended his right hand and Pearson shook it, feeling the strength in the grip.

'They're not welcome anywhere in Darworth, are they, Mr Kirkland?'

'Call me Steve.' The tattooed man smiled, and Pearson tried his best to smile back.

'Why are you here?' Kirkland wanted to know.

'I'm interested in what's happening in Darworth. The racial tension. I'm making a series of programmes about it.'

'I hope you tell the truth,' Kirkland told him.

'And what is the truth?'

'Yeah, there's problems here. There are in lots of places in this country. All over the world for that matter. But it's not all our fault, understand? It's not always us who are to blame. My brother was murdered by a fucking black and whoever did it still hasn't been caught. Do you know why? Because the police don't give a shit. If it was the other way round and it had been some nigger killed by a white guy they'd have turned the fucking place upside down to find the murderer.'

'You think the police in Darworth favour the black community?'

'Of course they do.'

'The blacks think otherwise. At least the ones I've spoken to do.'

'Which ones?'

'The ones up at the Western Road flats.'

'Why were you talking to them?'

'There was some trouble there last night.'

'What kind of trouble?' Kirkland asked, his face impassive.

'An arson attack,' Pearson continued, aware now that Kirkland was looking straight at him. 'A man was killed.'

'Do the police think that one of those bastards did it?'

'I think so. I spoke to the detective in charge of the investigation earlier today.'

'Martin Bishop. Yeah, I know him.'

Duggan and Carlton returned to the table, set down the drinks and seated themselves.

'Pity they weren't as interested when my brother Gary was murdered,' Kirkland went on.

'Do you know for sure he was killed by a black man?' Pearson asked.

'I was with him the night he died,' Duggan interjected.

'It's not always us to blame,' Kirkland said quietly. 'You go up to the cemetery, Copsley Fields, and have a look at what was done to some of the graves there. Graffiti sprayed on the gravestones of white people. Blacks did that. But do the law give a fuck?' He shook his head. 'My brother's grave's there too. You go and check it out.'

Pearson nodded and downed his drink in two large swallows.

'I've got to go,' he said. 'Work to do. Thanks for the drink.' He got to his feet.

'Don't forget,' Kirkland said. 'Tell the truth.'

Pearson nodded.

'See you around,' Kirkland called as the newsman headed out of the bar.

'Cunt,' muttered Duggan as he watched Pearson leave.

'Black cunt,' Carlton sneered.

'I can't believe you spoke to that bastard,' Duggan said, looking at Kirkland.

'He might come in handy,' the tattooed man said. 'A man with his pull. A man on the telly.'

'Come in handy for what?' Carlton wanted to know. 'Why should he help us?'

Kirkland smiled.

27

Nick Pearson set the laptop on the bedside table then crossed to the mini-bar in his room. He retrieved a bottle of orange juice and a glass then sat down on the edge of the bed and glanced at his e-mails.

Some spam. One from Gordon Dale. Another from Donna Greeling.

He opened that one first.

MOWENDE DISAPPEARS, it announced.

———

Dear Nick,

Further to my last e-mail about Victor Mowende, it seems that not only has he fled from Sierra Leone, he's disappeared off the face of the earth.

I haven't been able to find any info about him from anyone.

I know he was always clever and had loads of

contacts, but no one seems to know his where-abouts.

I'll keep my ears and eyes open. Hope you have more luck finding out something about him.

Love Donna.

———

Pearson sipped his orange juice, scanning the e-mail again. He waited a moment then opened the communication from Dale.

———

Nick,

How's it going? Hope the phone call this morning helped. Call me when you get five minutes.

Gordon.

———

Pearson nodded, finished his drink then headed towards the bathroom.

He felt as if he needed a shower. It had been a busy day, but also the time spent with Stephen Kirkland and his two cronies had left Pearson feeling grubby. He turned on the shower and watched the spray as he undressed, anxious to get beneath the purifying jets.

It was almost eight o'clock, he noted as he stepped beneath the water. After his shower he'd go down-stairs and have a meal in the hotel restaurant. After that he hadn't decided yet.

Drive round the estates again. Walk round Darworth town centre, see if there's anything happening after dark?

He closed his eyes and allowed the water to spatter his face.

The next morning he'd take a drive out to the cemetery that Kirkland had spoken of.

Might as well see as much as possible, eh?

In the bedroom, on the bedside table beside his laptop, his mobile phone began to ring.

Still in the shower, beneath the fierce jets of water, Pearson couldn't hear it.

It continued to ring for another few seconds then was silent.

28

The five black children were no older than ten.

They kicked the football around on the grass verge in front of the Western Road flats with an exuberance reserved only, it seemed, for youngsters of that age. An age when each day is the beginning of a new adventure.

As the sunset stained the clouds as surely as ink soaking into blotting paper, they shouted and laughed and ran around, calling to each other in their own languages. Occasionally one of them would look in the direction of the two burned-out vehicles that still stood in front of the flats, but for the most part they were content to play their game.

What had happened the previous night wasn't their concern. They had heard their parents talking about the fire. Two of them had even eavesdropped on conversations about a body found in the van. But now, as they ran and kicked their football around in the dying evening light, every other consideration was banished.

All that mattered was the game.

Younger children who had been playing with them had been called in by their parents and were now tucked up in bed. The remaining five knew that they too would be summoned by their parents very soon. So, as that collective realisation swept through them, they seemed to redouble their efforts, running faster, kicking the ball harder and shouting more loudly.

More than once the ball bounced into the road but, fortunately for the children, there wasn't much traffic about so one of them bounded on to the tarmac to retrieve it.

An old man walked past the flats, leading a small dog on a lead. Two of the children moved towards the animal, amused by its laboured waddling. It was grey around the muzzle, its tongue lolling from its mouth. The old man stopped and allowed the children to stroke the panting dog, and he smiled at the looks of delight on their faces.

The other three joined them and the whole group stood around looking at the dog for a moment longer until the old man waved and walked on, the dog struggling along beside him.

The five children went back to their game.

A misplaced kick, once again, sent the ball skidding into the road. The other four shouted mock insults at the kicker and told him to fetch it from where it had come to rest against the far kerb.

He ran across the grass, checked the road was clear, then hurried to retrieve the ball.

It was as he was walking back that the headlights cut through the gloom. Whether the car had been parked close by with its lights off or had driven by slowly without their noticing, the children could only guess.

Whatever the case, the air was suddenly filled with the sound of a roaring engine, and the vehicle shot forward as if fired from a cannon, lights blazing now.

The watching children screamed at their companion to get out of the road. One of them turned and ran back towards the flats to get help.

The boy in the road stood transfixed as the car bore down on him, pinning him in its headlights like an insect to a board. For precious seconds he couldn't move, but then something inside his mind seemed to force him into action. He ran for the safety of the pavement.

The car continued to hurtle straight at him.

29

The basement flats at Western Road had been empty the longest.

Each block had twelve subterranean dwellings but none had been inhabited for years. Darworth council had deemed them unfit for human habitation after a number of health and safety checks over the years, and as time had passed the flats below ground had become little more than dumping grounds for anything unwanted. Now even that use had been abandoned.

It was dark in the basements. The lights had long since ceased to function. Bulbs had been broken or taken and there was an absence of natural light because the outside windows had been bricked up. Doors were hanging off many of the main entrances. Paint peeled from walls like leprous flesh. The corridors were dirty, littered with mouse and rat droppings, but even the vermin themselves seemed unable to flourish in the filthy surroundings. There were decomposing rodent carcasses everywhere. The remains of a dead cat, its body seething with maggots, lay in the centre of one abandoned living room.

Insects seemed to survive with relative ease in the squalor. Cockroaches scuttled back and forth across the dirty floors. Spiders had adorned much of the basement with webs. There was a wasps' nest in one of the flats. And, everywhere, flies buzzed around, offering their own sound in the solitude.

Occasionally, children would venture down into the gloom via the concrete staircase, to test their courage more often than not. But, other than that, none of those who lived in the three blocks set foot in the basements.

Had they done so, they would have found that some of the flats had huge holes in their thin walls. Acts of mindless vandalism by the previous inhabitants, possibly? Two, sometimes three dwellings would be connected by crudely made breaches in the walls. The tools that had created these openings had usually been only sledgehammers wielded by unskilled hands.

It was as if those who had lived below ground before the Africans arrived had been a race of troglodytes. This had been their kingdom and, now they were gone, no one else wished to occupy it.

And yet, despite the filth and the stench of decay, the febrile air and the constantly buzzing flies, something sought refuge in this testament to neglect.

Oblivious of the swarms of insects, there was a presence in one of these long abandoned subterranean chambers. None saw it because it moved in darkness, more comfortable in the cloying gloom than in the light.

It shunned brightness now even more than it had previously.

Had the inhabitants of the Western Road flats known of its existence, they would have delighted in that fact at least. They would have thanked whichever gods they prayed to that it sought seclusion.

Indeed, had they realised its true nature, it is doubtful that any would have remained living above it.

Except for one.

30

'They will not help you.'

The tall African with the heavy-lidded eyes looked round at the faces before him, studying each with his piercing gaze.

He saw in their expressions that same look of awe and fear that he had seen on the faces of those he'd encountered in Madrid and, before that, Morocco.

He remembered every step of his journey but now he intended to stay where he was. For him, and for the hundreds of other Africans in these flats, Darworth was now home. The final stop on a trek that had brought him more than three thousand miles from his homeland.

'You should know that by now,' he continued. 'How long have you lived here? Long enough to know that you are hated and unwanted.'

Those who listened to his words realised that there was truth in them.

'The white policemen have no interest in you or your children,' the tall man continued. 'They will not help you.'

'Then who will?'

The question came from a man near the back of the room. Some of the others turned to look at him as if questioning the wisdom of his interjection.

'Who will help us if the white policemen do not?' the man continued. 'This is our country now.'

'Your country?' snorted the tall man dismissively. 'Look at the colour of your skin. Look in the mirror. This is not your country and it never will be. You are a fool if you think otherwise. If you belonged here would the whites try to kill your children?' He shook his head. 'Tonight, someone tried to kill five of your children.' The tall man pointed at the watching faces, his index finger moving slowly across all of them. 'Tried to run them down like dogs in the gutter. White men tried to do this. Be grateful they failed. *This* time they failed. Next time it might be different. Do you think white policemen are going to care? What are five fewer black faces to them?'

Some of those watching nodded in agreement but a heavy silence still hung over the room.

'I tried to help you,' the tall man went on angrily. 'Even before I arrived here.' He glared at the watching group. 'But you did not want my help then, did you?'

'We were afraid,' another voice offered.

134

'You have more reason to fear the whites than me,' the tall man snapped.

'What do you want us to do?' a third voice called.

'Fight back,' the tall man said. 'Do not rely on anyone but yourselves.'

'We cannot fight,' the third voice protested. 'We dare not spill white blood.'

'There are ways,' the tall man breathed, raising a hand to interrupt the speaker.

'Tell us,' the first man said.

The tall man smiled. 'You must trust me and only me. If you do not, then first your children will die. Then *you* will die.' He closed his eyes. 'This is as much a war as anything any of you saw in your homelands before you came here. The whites started this war against you. If you do not fight, they will continue until you are all dead or driven from this place. And if you are forced to leave here, then where will you go? Where else will you run?'

31

There were two entrances to the Copsley Fields cemetery. The newest, on the northern side of the vast
necropolis, comprised redbrick walls with wrought-
iron gates set into solid posts. It led on to a paved
driveway that snaked across the cemetery, past the
small contemporary chapel. Behind the chapel, marble
and metal markers on the carefully tended turf
commemorated those who had been cremated.

Across the driveway, headstones of white or black
marble indicated the final resting places of those
below them. Trees that had been planted barely ten
years earlier, when the cemetery was enlarged, grew
among the gravestones. A large expanse of land
reserved for future occupants stretched away towards
the high and immaculately trimmed privet hedge
that formed the perimeter.

The southern side of the cemetery was completely
different. It seemed to belong to another time.

One single large wooden gate, its timbers split and knotted, guarded a rutted walkway barely the width of a coffin. Above the gate there was a tall wooden construction that resembled a porch.

Huge oak trees, some hundreds of years old, towered above the low stone wall that formed the perimeter in this older sector. The same trees cast thick shadows across the overgrown grass that seemed intent on strangling the grave markers. Many of these monuments were so old and weathered it was impossible to make out the inscriptions upon them.

Tombs had collapsed in upon themselves. A number of stone crosses had fallen over and many of the graves were completely unmarked.

As Nick Pearson pushed his way past the wooden gate he couldn't help thinking that those who had once come to tend these old graves must themselves have been dead for some time now.

He could remember coming to such places as a child and collecting chestnuts by the dozen. The spiky husks of many recently fallen now lay rotting in the grass and on the pathway. He saw insects crawling over them. A bee buzzed lazily past him, landed on an old headstone, then took off again in its hunt for pollen.

Pearson saw a crane fly struggling in a large web spun between one of the oak trees and a battered and time-worn Celtic cross. He watched as a bloated spider advanced slowly upon the stricken insect.

Despite the early hour, the cool breeze that he

had felt when he clambered out of his car seemed not to reach him here. The air was heavy, almost oppressive, among the tall trees and overgrown grass.

The journalist stooped and picked up a fallen chestnut, pulling away the shell to reveal the shiny brown conker within. He slipped it into the pocket of his jacket and walked on. He passed a wooden hut that, he presumed, had once provided shelter for whoever had cared for this older part of the graveyard. Its windows were either broken or so filthy as to be opaque.

This side of Copsley Fields, he thought to himself, was as forgotten and neglected as those who rested in its earth.

Pearson walked slowly along the narrow path, glancing to his left and right. Up ahead he could see the tarmac driveway that seemed to act like a line of demarcation between the old and new sections of the cemetery. The massive oak trees were replaced by poplars as he approached the new side of Copsley Fields. The more recent graves were not shaded like the old ones, but instead bathed in daylight. The eastern side looked almost welcoming compared to the dank and overgrown part through which Pearson had come. He quickened his pace as he drew nearer to the tarmac driveway.

But it was something closer at hand that caught his attention.

Off to his left, among the older graves.

For a moment, Pearson thought it was some kind

of bizarre monument. A grave marker that belonged to a bygone age.

As he moved off the path towards it, he saw that it was not.

The long, dew-soaked grass seemed to clutch at his feet as he walked between the older graves. He tripped over one of them, dislodging the rusted metal vase and almost losing his footing.

Only a few feet in front of him now was the object that had drawn his gaze.

'Jesus Christ,' he murmured, the words catching in his throat.

32

It took Pearson a moment or two to realise that there were portions of at least three corpses propped on top of the white marble headstone.

As he took a step nearer, he saw that the rotting bodies were arranged like some kind of macabre sculpture fashioned from putrescent flesh and splintered bones.

The corpse of a man sat upright on the headstone, held in place by a long piece of tree branch. One end of the branch was wedged into the ground, the other, the one that supported the body, was jammed into the decayed lumbar region of the cadaver.

Pearson surveyed the scene before him, his nostrils catching the rancid stench that was coming from the twisted forms.

On one knee, the body of the man cradled the severed head of a woman. Pearson could see that it was a woman because the features were still relatively intact. Both eyes were closed and there was dark fluid seeping from the nostrils, mouth and ears but there was some hair still upon the scalp and the face had not yet decayed enough to disguise its sex.

He wondered for a second where the rest of the corpse might be.

The body that lay across the lap of the dead man was unmistakably that of a child. Pearson guessed, from its height alone, that it was nine or ten. A boy. He also presumed that the body had not been buried for very long because the putrefaction was minimal. The eyeballs had become liquescent, but apart from that, and some discoloration around the cheeks and neck, the small body was in reasonable condition.

The journalist reached into the pocket of his jacket and pulled out his camera. He took six shots of the bodies from various angles, then slid the Nikon back into his pocket and gazed more intently at the monstrous sculpture of rotten flesh that confronted him.

He glanced at the cracked gravestone beside him and read the inscription aloud: 'Frances Hutchens. Died 1937.'

The engraving on the one to his right was more difficult to read because of the moss that had spread over the stone, but Pearson deciphered it anyway.

'Henry Nyles. Died 1940,' he murmured.

Considering this was the older part of the grave-yard, Pearson thought, none of the bodies looked as if it had been disinterred from this section. Any corpse taken from these resting places would have been little more than bone by now.

Taken from.

The full impact of those words struck him hard.

Three corpses have been dug up. Lifted from their graves and carried to this part of the cemetery. Three graves have been robbed.

He watched a fly crawl into one of the oozing nostrils of the severed head.

Grave robbing? What the fuck is this? Burke and Hare strike again? Even the term 'grave robbing' sounds archaic.

He walked on quickly, anxious to leave the nightmarish vision behind him. The smell was also becoming intolerable.

To the right of the path there was another body.

It was a man. That much was obvious from his clothing.

The body was draped, head down, over a time-ravaged headstone. Pearson approached it slowly and saw that, like the other corpses, this one was not in an advanced state of decomposition. It too must have come from the newer part of the cemetery.

He stood only feet away from it, gazing at the back of the neck.

There were several cross-shaped wounds in the slimy flesh. To Pearson, they looked as if they were fresh. Bone gleamed whitely through one of the lacerations.

He took more photos, his breath now rasping in his lungs, his nostrils clogged with the stench of decay.

He realised that he had reached the driveway

separating the two sides of the necropolis, and from where he stood he could see piles of dark earth surrounding a grave on the other side of the tarmac.

One of those disturbed.

He dug his hand in his pocket, pulled out his mobile phone and called up the number Bishop had given him.

As he waited for his call to be answered, he continued to gaze around the cemetery. He wondered how many more graves had been tampered with, how many more corpses had been pulled from their resting places.

Nearby a large black crow landed on a stone cross and hungrily eyed the body before it. Pearson flapped his hand angrily at the carrion-feeder and it rose into the air only to circle and land again a little further away. It fixed him in its gaze, its loud cawing attracting others.

He knew they'd be descending to feed on the other bodies in no time.

Pearson held on to the phone and waited.

33

'What were you doing here?'

Pearson heard the words, but for a second they seemed not to register. He continued to gaze raptly at the body of the man still draped across the headstone.

Two forensics men dressed from head to foot in white overalls were moving carefully around it.

In other parts of the cemetery, the same kind of inspection was being repeated where other corpses had been found and where graves had been disturbed.

'Mr Pearson,' Detective Sergeant Martin Bishop said again, placing one hand on the journalist's arm.

'Sorry,' Pearson exclaimed, shaking his head as if to dispel the trance he seemed to have fallen into. 'I came to look at the cemetery. Something to do with the story I'm working on. I saw the bodies, so I called you.'

'Did you see anyone around?'

'No. What the hell's going on?'

'That's what we're trying to find out.'

'How many graves have been disturbed?'

'Nine as far as we can tell. Seven bodies were actually removed. Two other graves were dug up but the bodies weren't taken out.'

'Were they all from the newer side of the cemetery?'

'It looks like it.'

'What about the ones that weren't removed? Was anything done to them?'

'Like what?'

'Like the mutilation on the back of the neck.'

Bishop nodded ruefully. 'All the corpses had the same marks somewhere on them,' he said. 'Even the severed head you saw back there.' He gestured over his shoulder towards the older part of Copsley Fields. 'The marks were cut into the left cheek.'

'Any link between the bodies in the graves that were desecrated?' Pearson asked.

'It's too early to tell until we run a proper check but it doesn't look like it. It seems as if the desecrations were random.'

'So someone got in here last night, dug up nine graves, mutilated the corpses and took seven of them out of their coffins.'

'That's what it looks like.'

Pearson sighed wearily and glanced around him once again.

All over the cemetery plain clothes and uniformed police moved among the headstones. Forensics experts, in those distinctive white overalls, wandered about sweating in the midday heat.

'What about the bodies?' the journalist asked. 'What are you going to do with them?'

'They'll be examined here for fingerprints, identified and then reburied,' Bishop told him. 'The relatives will be informed.'

He reached for a cigarette and lit it. Pearson accepted the one he was offered.

'One of the disturbed graves belonged to Stephen Kirkland's brother,' he said. 'I wonder who he's going to blame?'

'How do you know Kirkland?'

'I met him in the George and Dragon yesterday. He said that graffiti had been sprayed on some of the graves here. That's why I was here this morning, to see if he was telling the truth.'

'I wouldn't have thought Stephen Kirkland would have confided in you, Mr Pearson,' the detective observed.

'Because I'm black?'

'Yeah.'

'Well he did. I think he wants to make sure his side gets heard too.'

The two men picked their way back to the pathway and wandered in the direction of the older part of the cemetery.

'The marks on the bodies,' Bishop continued. 'I've

seen them before. That guy we found burned up in the van outside the Western Road flats the other day, he had them too.'

Pearson looked quizzically at the detective. 'Why are you telling me? In fact, why are you telling me any of this?'

'Because I need all the fucking help I can get,' Bishop said flatly.

Pearson smiled.

'The weird thing, and this mustn't go any further,' Bishop continued, 'is that his body's missing. As far as we can tell, it was stolen from the morgue after the post-mortem was carried out.'

'You think it's linked to what's happened here?'

'If you pushed me, I'd say it's likely.'

Pearson nodded then took a long drag on his cigarette.

'The marks on the bodies,' he said quietly. 'I've seen them before. Five years ago, I was working in Liberia, doing a story about the arms trade. Guys there were making millions selling old Russian equipment to both sides in the civil war. I went to a village to report on some inter-tribal massacre. Every one of the bodies we found had those same symbols carved into the backs of their necks.'

34

'So you're telling me that Africans did this?' Bishop demanded.

'I didn't say that,' Pearson protested. 'I just told you that the last time I saw marks like the ones on the bodies in this cemetery was on corpses in Liberia. That might not mean anything.'

'No, you're right, it might not. But it's something.'

'But what I saw was in Liberia.'

'And I said that the African refugees in this town came from every country on that continent. Who's to say some of them aren't from Liberia?'

'Even if they are it doesn't mean they're responsible for what's happened here,' Pearson protested.

'If they didn't do anything they've got nothing to worry about, have they?'

'If you keep dragging them in, they're going to start screaming police harassment. Then this racial situation you've got is really going to blow up.'

'What the fuck do you suggest I do? A few days ago I find a dead African incinerated in a van outside the Western Road flats. That same body is covered in markings, symbols identical to the ones on the corpses we've found here. Only this time, it's the corpses of white people, pulled from their graves and mutilated.' He took a final drag on his cigarette and stamped it out under his shoe.

'So what happened here is worse than the murder and disappearance of one black man?'

'Oh, for Christ's sake,' Bishop said wearily. 'Give me a break, Pearson. The two crimes look as if they're linked. It's my job to find out if they are.' He ran a hand through his hair. 'If this gets out, if the relatives of the people who were dug up think that a bunch of African refugees are responsible, I'll have a full scale fucking race war on my hands. What Stephen Kirkland and his little mob have pulled so far will look like a picnic. There'll be people signing up for the fucking Ku Klux Klan in the main street of Darworth. Now you tell me what I'm supposed to do.'

'What if it's not the locals who start fighting?' Pearson demanded. 'What if it's the Africans? They're the ones being persecuted.'

'They're not being persecuted,' Bishop snapped. 'They're being questioned.'

'You sound as if you want it to be them,' Pearson told him, an accusatory edge to his voice.

'You were the one who told me you saw those marks on African bodies,' said the detective.

149

'That still doesn't mean the ones here in Darworth are responsible for these desecrations.'

'Then when I've questioned them and I'm satisfied that they're not, I'll go looking for the people who *did* do this.' He gestured around him.

Pearson regarded him evenly for a moment.

'Have you got any idea what the marks mean?' Bishop enquired. 'If they signify anything?'

'I can find out.'

'Will you do that for me? Find out if those symbols are religious or tribal or something. I'm asking for your help. If you want to give it, that's great. If not, then just stay out of the way. Because I'm going to be busy.'

Pearson regarded the policeman warily then he too dropped the butt of his cigarette, hearing it hiss on the long, still damp grass.

'I'll call you when I've got something,' he said. 'Meanwhile, here's my card.'

He turned and headed back along the path towards his waiting car.

As he passed the monstrous sculpture of decaying bodies and limbs perched on the gravestone, the stink of rotting flesh assaulted his nostrils once again. The crows that had been gathering in the trees for some time continued to screech loudly.

To Pearson, their cries sounded like mocking laughter.

35

In his hotel room, Nick Pearson sipped at the cup of tea he'd made and allowed his gaze to flick back and forth over the screen of the laptop.

The attachment had arrived five minutes earlier from Gordon Dale. He'd even added some photographs that Pearson himself had taken at the time.

SLAUGHTER OF THE INNOCENTS screamed the headline on the piece. It was dated 9 July, five years earlier.

Pearson clicked on one of the photos. It showed a shallow pit, choked with the bodies of men, women and children. All African. All riddled with bullets.

The journalist maximised the image and leaned closer to the screen.

'Bingo,' he murmured.

He drew one index finger over the picture before him. On the back of the necks of three of the victims were the same symbols he'd seen that morning on the corpses at Copsley Fields.

Liberia five years ago. Darworth today. What the fuck is going on?

No one, he recalled, had ever been brought to justice for the massacre in that village. But then, very few of the crimes against humanity perpetrated during the countless civil wars in Africa had ever been adequately punished.

Pearson looked at the photo again. At the symbols.

Coincidence?

Two different continents. Five years between the events. He shook his head.

Same perpetrator?

Part of his job, he'd always thought, was to retain a healthy scepticism regarding things such as coincidence.

Is this any different?

Was it really such a stretch of credibility, such a leap of faith, to think that the same person or persons responsible for the massacre in that Liberian village five years ago could now be living in this little town in England?

He exhaled and rubbed his eyes. Then he opened another file and discovered several more shots taken at the scene of the slaughter. He maximised each in turn, shaking his head as he noticed that the symbols were again clear on the necks of a number of the victims.

He was still pondering on their nature when his mobile phone rang.

'Hello,' he said into the mouthpiece, his eyes still on the laptop's screen.

'Nick. It's Gordon Dale. That stuff about the massacre in Liberia, was it any help?'

'Yeah, thanks, Gordon. I'm looking at it now.'

'What's going on there?'

'I haven't quite figured that out yet,' Pearson admitted, still gazing at the screen of the laptop. 'By the way, Gordon, did you know that Victor Mowende's on the run? I heard yesterday.'

'I saw something about it. Wasn't Mowende implicated in that massacre? The one I sent you the stuff about?'

'Yes, that one and dozens of others like it.'

'He tried to kill you, didn't he?'

Pearson nodded to himself. 'About six years ago, in Sierra Leone. I got a little too close to him,' he said quietly. 'Thanks for this stuff, Gordon. I'll call you later.'

He terminated the call, put down the mobile and returned his attention to the screen, clicking on another picture. The bodies in that one also bore the same cuts on the back of the neck.

The journalist sipped at his tea.

Despite the fact that it was warm in the room, he felt the hairs on his forearms stand up.

36

Banks of rain-swollen cloud moved menacingly across the horizon. DS Bishop lit his cigarette and watched them gathering. Beside him, DC Hall leaned on the concrete balustrade and looked out from the third floor of the block.

'How many have we spoken to so far?' the younger man sighed. 'Thirty? Forty? And no one's told us anything worth hearing.'

Bishop took another drag on his cigarette and continued to gaze at the dark clouds.

'How are we supposed to know for sure if they're telling the truth?' Hall persisted. 'Even the ones who can speak English.'

'We've got to keep trying, Dan.'

'Then perhaps we'd better get that interpreter back who helped us before.'

'Perhaps we're just asking the wrong questions.' Bishop shrugged. 'I mean, we can't expect them to give us the answers we want when we're not even sure what we're looking for. "Excuse me, but have you ever indulged in body snatching or grave dese-cration?" That'd be more to the point, wouldn't it?'

'Don't bite my head off, guv, but the only reason we're interviewing these people is because some newsman once saw similar marks on some corpses in Africa, right?'

'Marks exactly the same as the ones on the bodies we found dug up at Copsley Fields, yeah. We're interviewing them because it's the only fucking lead we've got.'

The DS finished his cigarette and dropped the butt over the balustrade.

'Come on,' he said wearily. 'Let's get on with it.'

The figure that loomed into view as they turned startled them both.

He was a tall, powerfully built black man with heavy-lidded eyes. His hands were like ham hocks.

He regarded the two policemen silently for a moment, looking appraisingly at them.

'You are policemen,' he said finally. His voice was low and gravelly but his diction was close to perfect. The words sounded like a statement rather than a question.

'Yes, we are.' Bishop reached for his ID.

'Do you live here, sir?' Hall added, also flipping open the slim leather wallet that held his own identification.

The tall man nodded. 'There have been many

policemen here today,' he said. 'And yet you still come. Why?'

'There are questions we need to ask,' Bishop explained.

'Have you asked others?' the tall man enquired. 'Or just the people who live here? My people?'

'Your people?' Bishop said quizzically.

'Africans.'

'This isn't a racial matter.'

'Perhaps it is,' the tall man answered. 'Have you spoken to the white men who tried to kill five of our children last night?'

'When?' Bishop wanted to know. 'We had no reports of any trouble here.'

'That's because nothing was said,' the tall man insisted. 'There would have been no point.'

'How did they try to kill five children?' Bishop demanded.

'They drove a car at them, Detective.'

'You should have notified us,' Hall offered.

'For what reason?' the tall man said dismissively. 'You would have done nothing. As you have done nothing to protect my people these past few months.'

'That's not true,' Bishop said defensively. 'My men have done everything in their power to stop racist attacks against the residents of these flats.'

'Then why are so many of the windows here broken?' the tall man said challengingly. 'It was white men who threw the stones that smashed them. It was white men who sprayed insults on the walls.

Whites who burned the cars down there.' He jabbed a finger over the balustrade. 'Where were your men when that happened, Detective?'

Bishop held up a hand as if to silence the newcomer.

'Before we go any further,' he said evenly, 'would you mind telling us your name, please, sir?'

'My name is Mowende,' the tall man told him. 'Victor Mowende.'

37

'How do you know it was white men who tried to kill the children?' DS Bishop asked. 'Did someone see them?'

Mowende looked at each of the policemen in turn, then sneered.

'No one saw white men spraying graffiti on these walls or setting fire to the cars either,' he said. 'But we all know they did.'

'Attempted murder is a serious charge, Mr Mowende,' Bishop pointed out. 'If you want to make an official complaint—'

The tall man raised a hand to silence him. 'As I said, nothing would be done anyway.'

'You seem very sure of that,' Bishop countered.

'How long have you lived here, Mr Mowende?' Hall asked.

'Long enough,' the tall man told him.

'Where were you born? Which country did you leave to come here?' Bishop wanted to know.

'I am African.'

'Africa's a big continent, Mr Mowende,' the DS reminded him. 'I was hoping you'd be more specific.'

'I have lived in many places, Detective.'

'And now you find yourself in our country,' Bishop said.

'Along with thousands of my people. We didn't ask to be here. All we want is to live our lives in peace. But your people will not let us. Why are you here?'

'We need to ask some questions,' Bishop told him. 'Some graves were disturbed at the local cemetery.'

'So you blame us for that. Blame the blacks,' Mowende snapped.

'This is part of our inquiry, Mr Mowende,' the DS explained. 'We have reason to believe that someone living here might know something about what happened at the cemetery.'

'What makes you think that?'

'There were marks on the dug-up bodies that are similar to those found on African corpses in Liberia,' Bishop said evenly. 'It's possible that the person responsible now lives in these flats. Have you ever lived in Liberia, Mr Mowende?'

'I told you, Detective. I have lived in lots of places during my life.'

'What brought you here?'

'A need for safety,' the African said, smiling crookedly. 'From persecution. It is unfortunate that I seem to have chosen the wrong place to settle.'

'Do you know many of the other residents of these flats?' Bishop asked.

Mowende nodded.

'What about a man called Emmanuel Agassa?' the DS persisted. 'His body disappeared from the local hospital. It was marked in the same way as those we found at the cemetery. The same as the ones in Africa.'

'You think that some deaths in Liberia, some grave robbing in your little town and a missing body are all linked?' Mowende laughed.

'That's what we're trying to find out, yes,' Bishop told him. 'I'm pleased you find it amusing, Mr Mowende. We're just doing our job.'

'No one here knows anything,' the African snapped, his grin fading rapidly.

'Well, when we've spoken to them we'll be able to decide if you're right or not,' the DS told him. 'Perhaps you'd like to help us. After all, a lot of your people don't speak very good English, do they? The quicker they answer our questions the quicker we can leave them in peace. Perhaps you could act as an interpreter for us.'

Mowende regarded the detective warily for a moment; then he nodded almost imperceptibly.

'I will help you,' he declared.

38

'Come on, Gemma. No one's going to see us.'

Craig Finn smiled broadly and grabbed Gemma Hill's hand, pulling her towards the main gates of the Copsley Fields cemetery.

'I'm not going in there,' she giggled, trying to wriggle free of his grip.

'Go on,' he urged. 'We can't go to your house because of your mum and dad. And my house is miles away. *And* my sister's in tonight. At least it's quiet in there.' He inclined his head towards the necropolis.

'It's also cold, Craig,' she protested.

'I'll keep you warm,' he muttered, pulling her closer to him.

They kissed deeply for a moment and she giggled again as she felt him close one hand over her right breast. He squeezed hard and she yelped and stepped back.

'Not so rough,' she chided, punching him on the arm.

'Are we going in, then?' Finn persisted, hooking a thumb towards the main gates of the cemetery.

'The vicar only lives over there,' she protested, pointing towards a small detached house on the other side of the road. There was a light burning in one of the downstairs rooms. 'If he comes over and finds us we'll be in trouble.'

'He won't find us,' Finn reassured her. 'He's too busy reading his Bible or something.' He slipped his hand beneath her short black skirt, raking his fingers over the cotton of her panties. 'Come on. I'm really horny.' He grabbed her hand and pressed it to the erection that was straining against the crotch of his jeans. 'See?'

'So am I,' she told him, pulling away again. 'But I'm not horny enough to shag in a cemetery.'

He leered. 'You will be.'

'You're a pervert,' she giggled. 'Wanting to do it surrounded by dead bodies.'

'Oh, come on, we've done it everywhere else. On a bus. In your mum and dad's bed. In the toilet at that club.'

'That was my favourite,' she sighed wistfully. 'Especially when we knew those two girls were outside listening.'

'Well, this will be even better.' He turned and headed for the gates.

'How are we going to get in?'

'Just climb over the wall. I'll give you a leg up.'

He stood by the redbrick perimeter, his hands clasped together, fingers interlocked, waiting for her.

Gemma hesitated for a moment then slipped off her shoes and placed one bare foot on Finn's hands.

'Ready?' he grunted and lifted her.

She yelped as she rose into the air, her hands scrabbling at the top of the wall.

'Shh,' he hissed.

'Well, I'm falling,' she protested.

'Just pull yourself over,' he snapped, lifting her higher.

She landed with a thud on the other side.

'Shit,' she groaned. 'I think I've bruised my arse.'

Smiling to himself, Finn took a jump at the wall and hauled himself upwards, hooking one leg over the top and dragging his weight to the top. He sat on the wall, glancing back across the road at the house opposite. The single light still burned in the downstairs room.

He dropped down on the other side, almost colliding with Gemma.

'It's muddy, you dickhead,' she protested. 'My clothes will be ruined. This skirt was expensive, you know.'

He slid his arm round her waist, ignoring her protests.

'I'll make it up to you,' he said, kissing her cheek.

'You'd better,' she told him huskily, squeezing his backside. 'You can start now.'

She pulled him towards her and they kissed fiercely.

He slipped one hand between her legs again, pushing his fingers past the gusset of her panties until they brushed her cleft. He stroked her gently, feeling her moisture on his fingers, allowing two of the probing digits to glide between her swollen labial lips.

'The grass isn't the only thing that's wet.' He smiled, his breath coming in short gasps.

'Let's go over there,' she breathed, gesturing towards the older part of the cemetery.

Finn slid his fingers free and pressed them to her mouth. She licked at her own wetness then sucked his fingers hard into her mouth.

'Fucking hell,' he gasped.

They moved quickly across the gravel drive, Gemma yelping in discomfort as the stones dug into her bare feet. Finn swept her slim form up into his arms and carried her. She laughed and he was forced to quieten her once again.

'I thought you didn't want to get caught,' he muttered. 'The vicar will hear if you don't shut up.'

'I don't care any more.'

Finn put her down as they reached the other side of the drive. She felt the wet grass beneath her feet once again as they walked on.

'Over there,' she said suddenly, pulling him along with her.

As they moved further away from the perimeter wall, the light from the street lamps diminished. By the time they stopped running, they could only see a yard ahead of them.

'On there,' Gemma said, pointing at a flat marble stone set into the ground. 'Put your jacket down.'

He pulled off his padded jacket and laid it on the marble. Gemma reached up beneath her skirt and tugged at her knickers, sliding them down her slender thighs and wriggling out of them. Then she dropped to her knees in front of him and tugged at his zip, freeing his erection. As it waved stiffly before her she ran two nails along its length before closing her mouth over the swollen head.

'Fuck,' Finn gasped, stroking her hair.

With his penis still in her mouth, Gemma unbuttoned his jeans and tugged them down as far as his knees, cupping his testicles in her free hand. Her head continued to move slowly back and forth, her mouth working on his erection.

Finn closed his eyes, aware only of the wonderful sensations she was arousing.

'Go on,' he murmured throatily.

'My turn now,' she said, pulling her mouth away from his penis. He looked down to see that his shaft was covered in her saliva.

She remained on her knees but turned away from him, arching her back so that her buttocks were pointing up at him. Finn got on his knees behind her and parted her legs a little further. Then he pushed his face towards her sex, flicking his tongue over her puckered anus and into the hot wetness of her vagina.

'Just fuck me,' she told him breathlessly.

He pressed his stiffness against her for a moment then allowed the shaft to slide into her. They both gasped.

Finn gripped her hips and began thrusting slowly. She pushed back hard against each of his movements, wanting him deeper inside her. He saw that she was now supporting her weight on just one hand as the fingers of the other rubbed her swollen clitoris.

'Go on,' she moaned. 'God, that's good.'

He pushed into her hard and held himself there, his hands raking her back.

'Don't fucking stop,' she panted imploringly, looking over her shoulder. 'What's wrong?'

'I thought I heard something,' Finn told her, his own breath coming in gasps, his erection still deep inside her.

'Like what?'

'I don't know. It was probably just an owl or something.'

'Or the vicar. Perhaps he's watching us.'

Finn smiled and prepared to continue, but suddenly froze again.

'Listen,' he said urgently.

166

'Yeah, very funny, Craig. Now stop trying to scare me and just carry on, will you?'

'I wasn't trying to scare you,' he protested. 'I heard something.'

'Good for you,' she breathed. 'Well, if you just get on with it you *will* hear something in a minute. The sound of me coming.' As if to reinforce her words she pushed her buttocks back against him.

He started to thrust into her again, and away to his right there was a rustling sound high above him.

The owl came hurtling out of one of the poplars and sped across the cemetery less than ten feet from the ground.

'Fucking hell,' Finn gasped as he saw the bird hurtle past him.

It dived towards the ground and he heard a high-pitched squeal. Seconds later, the owl rose into the air again, something small and bloody clutched in its claws.

'Shit,' Finn grunted, slipping backwards.

His penis slid out of Gemma, who peered irritably back over her shoulder at him.

'Now what?' she panted.

'It was an owl,' he said apologetically. 'I think it got a mouse or something. That must have been what I heard before.'

'That's great, Craig,' Gemma said sardonically, her bottom still sticking up invitingly before him. 'Now, if there's nothing else . . .'

He smiled and knelt behind her once more.

In the darkness away to their right something else moved near the trees. Something much bigger than an owl.

39

The Reverend Duncan Carraway muttered irritably to himself as he hurried towards the downstairs lavatory, certain that he was going to wet himself.

He pushed open the door, grabbed at the cord that operated the light and blundered in. Unzipping hastily, he stood awaiting the stream of urine he felt he had to release.

Nothing happened.

To his dismay there was no outpouring. No feeling of relief as he emptied his bladder.

Four or five drops of dark urine dribbled into the bowl below, but apart from that there was nothing.

He tutted and shook himself, returning irritably to the sitting room.

This kind of thing had happened too many times lately: the raging desire to urinate followed only by the disappointment and discomfort he'd just experienced. Carraway was certain he knew what the problem was. He had prostate trouble. After all, he reasoned, he was fifty-six. It was the kind of age when that type of malady afflicted a man.

He sat down heavily in his chair, exhaling wearily. He had no choice now but to visit the doctor, and he feared the worst.

Prostate trouble. Prostate cancer, possibly?

He tried to force the thought from his mind and, instead, concentrate on the work at hand. He glanced down at his notes.

> *Set up for group*
> *Arrival of parents and children*
> *Playtime with toys*
> *Singing session*
> *Art and craft*
> *Tea and juice*

Carraway smiled to himself. It was the same routine every time for his ABC group.

Adults, babies and children. He had thought of it himself. The group met every Tuesday and Thursday at the church hall in his parish. He himself oversaw the singing session, strumming away on his acoustic guitar like a kind of ecclesiastical Johnny Cash. He checked the list of songs for the following day then, to his dismay, felt that he would have to visit the lavatory again.

He decided to wait. Perhaps if he did he would

actually be able to empty his bladder when he finally went. Carraway wandered from the sitting room through to the kitchen where he switched on the kettle and dropped a camomile tea bag into a mug on the worktop.

He hoped it would help him sleep. Sleep, like the ability to urinate properly, was something that had been eluding him lately. He wondered if the two were linked but quickly dismissed his own diagnosis.

If he was honest with himself, it had been the incident in the cemetery the previous night that had upset him so much. The desecrations. He shook his head in dismay just at the recollection of it.

How could anyone be so callous? So unfeeling? He glanced across the room at a crucifix, looking intently at the small figure of Christ that hung upon it. To the vicar it seemed as if some kind of divine intervention was needed to explain the actions of those who would defile the last resting place of a man, woman or child.

The kettle boiled and Carraway made his tea, then headed back towards the sitting room with it.

He was in the hallway when he heard the scratching at the front door.

Carraway hesitated, listening to the scrabbling. It sounded like nails against the wood. He took a step towards the door then stopped when the noise ceased.

Silence.

He turned and headed back towards the sitting room once more. As he reached the threshold, the sound of three loud bangs on the front door caused him to turn once again.

He looked at his watch, wondering who would be calling on him at ten forty-five at night, then crossed to the front door and stood looking at it.

Three more bangs startled him and he almost spilled the tea he still carried. Setting the cup down on a nearby table, he leaned towards the door.

'Hello,' he called.

No answer.

He reached for the lock and gently released it, noticing that the security light over the porch was on. It was triggered by movement. Someone had been outside. Perhaps they still were.

He opened the door and peered out into the night.

Nothing.

Perhaps a cat had triggered the light. But even if it had, he reasoned, a cat couldn't have banged on the front door the way he'd heard.

Carraway stepped out on to the porch and took a couple of paces along the short paved path that led to the pavement beyond.

He looked in both directions but saw no one.

A car drove past, breaking the silence. But the vicar could see nobody walking.

So, who banged on the door?

He shook his head and retreated back into the

hall, locking and bolting the front door. The security light went out, plunging the front of the house into darkness once more.

Someone playing some kind of stupid joke, perhaps? Carraway thought. He shook his head wearily. Then he retrieved his tea and headed for the sitting room.

Outside, the security light came on again.

40

The slight breeze that had sprung up brought the first hint of the smell to Craig Finn's nostrils.

He slowed his thrusts slightly, wrinkling his nose at the odour.

On all fours in front of him, Gemma Hill felt the urgency of his strokes decrease. She moaned softly in protest.

Finn increased his speed again, conscious that his own climax was building now. Gemma was pushing back harder against him with each deep penetration. He pushed her skirt up so that it was around her waist, looking down to admire her taut buttocks and to watch his erection sliding in and out of her sex.

But still he could not breathe without that tainted air filling his nostrils. It smelled like decaying waste left untended beneath sunshine. And now the stench was becoming so powerful he was finding it almost impossible to take the deep breaths he needed.

Again he slowed down, content to merely rest his erection inside Gemma.

'Oh, for fuck's sake, Craig,' she breathed. 'Now what? Are you doing this on purpose?'

He coughed and took one hand from her hips to shield his nose and mouth.

'That fucking smell,' he grunted.

Gemma was about to protest when she too became aware of the noxious odour.

'Let's just finish and go back to my house,' she suggested, also coughing from the fetid stink that seemed to be all around them now like an invisible cloud.

Craig began pushing into her quickly, holding his breath when he could to prevent himself from inhaling the choking fumes.

'Go on,' she panted encouragingly, also trying to take shallow breaths to minimise the effect of the vile odour.

'Fuck it, I can't,' he snapped, pulling his penis free of the welcoming embrace of her moist cleft. 'That smell is fucking disgusting.'

Gemma turned to say something to him but the words dissolved into a scream.

In the tenebrous gloom of the cemetery she could see a figure standing only inches behind Finn. Reaching for him.

'What?' He gaped at her.

The figure lunged towards him.

Gemma scrambled backwards, her eyes bulging madly in their sockets, the smell now intolerable.

Finn saw a shape rise from behind a gravestone to Gemma's left. A form that seemed to detach itself from the dark night air. He managed to shout a warning before he felt hands round his throat, fingers pressing into his larynx and squeezing with incredible power.

Gemma hauled herself upright only to be dragged down again by the shape close by, which shot out a hand and gripped her wrist, pulling her to the ground. She lost her balance and cracked her temple on a headstone as she fell. A small cut began weeping blood down one side of her face.

But the terror kept her conscious and now she was aware of a weight pressing down on her. Hands were closing round her neck. Thumbs pressed in on her windpipe with the force of a vice.

Somewhere in the darkness she heard Finn choking. There was a loud crack that reminded her of a snapping tree branch. She didn't realise it was Finn's neck.

All she was aware of now was the crushing weight upon her, the monstrous stench in her nostrils and the hands that clawed at every part of her body.

She struggled against the attack but fear paralysed her as effectively as the figure that held her down. White stars danced before her eyes as she fought for breath. She tasted blood in her mouth and realised she had bitten through her own tongue.

And, all the time, that foul stench of decay filled her nostrils. Her stomach contracted violently and she was convinced she was going to vomit.

She kicked out madly but the blows had no effect on her attackers and the impact became weaker as she felt the strength seeping from her.

She wanted to scream for help. Wanted to ask these figures why they were killing her. Tears began to roll from her eyes, a combination of pain and fearful realisation. The monstrous scene swam before her and she knew she was close to blacking out. Then, for a split second, everything was bathed in a red sheen as one of the blood vessels in her left eye burst. Her kicks ceased.

The hands round her throat continued to squeeze.

41

There must be a cat in the garden. It was the only explanation that the Reverend Duncan Carraway could come up with.

It had to be a cat that he could hear moving around near the bushes outside. Either that or a hedgehog. Carraway sipped at his camomile tea and wondered whether or not he should leave a saucer of water out just in case it was a hedgehog. He finally decided against it.

He yawned and thought that it was time to retire to bed. He felt pleasantly drowsy (a result of the camomile tea, he told himself) and ready for sleep. Now if he could only manage to empty his bladder without pain before he got into bed, he would feel much better.

He switched off the lights in the sitting room and made his way towards the stairs.

As he reached the bottom of the steps he noticed two things.

First, a strong odour in the hallway. A revolting smell that brought to mind rotting meat.

Second, there was something on the third step up. Carraway leaned forward and picked it up. He was surprised to find that it was compacted earth.

There was more on the step above. Had he brought it in on his shoes earlier that day?

He glanced across to the area close to the front door where he kept his footwear. His wellington boots and both pairs of shoes there were clean. He shook his head in puzzlement.

Perhaps some mud had stuck to his slippers when he'd gone out to investigate the banging on the door? He dismissed the theory immediately. He hadn't been upstairs since his little foray outside into the night.

Carraway shrugged. Perhaps it had been there all day and he just hadn't noticed. A word with his cleaner in the morning might be prudent.

He climbed the stairs, the smell growing stronger as he went.

That certainly hadn't been there earlier.

The vicar wondered if the upstairs lavatory might be blocked. It wouldn't be the first time.

He reached the landing, finding it difficult to breathe because the smell was so intense, and headed towards the lavatory. He pushed open the door.

The smell was less intense inside the small room. As he stood there preparing to urinate he glanced down into the bowl and saw that there was no blockage. The foul stench was not being caused by sewage.

He waited for the stream of urine but, predictably, none came. The vicar sighed wearily and washed his hands, heading out on to the landing once again.

The smell was still there. Thick and cloying. It was so strong it was practically palpable. He passed across the landing to his own bedroom, where the stench was virtually intolerable.

Carraway decided that it would be easier to sleep in the spare room for tonight. He was tired and he didn't feel like tracking down the source of the mysterious and fetid odour now. He would get a good night's sleep then find the cause of it in the morning.

As he looked quickly round the room, however, something else puzzled him. He had hung a crucifix above his bed. A wood and metal one about twenty centimetres long.

It was missing.

He turned back towards the landing, and as he did so, a figure rose from beside the bed.

Carraway never saw it.

And even if he heard its footfalls as it swiftly drew nearer to him, he had no time to turn.

Hands grabbed him by the throat and he tried to shout out in fear and pain but the cry was cut short by the pressure on his windpipe.

The stench in his nostrils intensified. And, in that split second, he thought he knew what it was. It was something he'd experienced before, only not as intensely as this.

It was the smell of death.

The fact had barely registered with him when he felt his head being driven forward at speed, and his forehead was slammed against the bedroom door with such force that he almost blacked out.

With his head spinning from the impact, and also from the lack of air as the choking hands gripped him even more tightly, he felt his knees give out but he didn't fall. The hands kept him upright. He remained on his feet, supported by that grip but dying because of it.

Then, suddenly, it was released.

Carraway dropped to his knees, reaching feebly for his throat. He tried to cough but could only make a rasping noise that sounded as if he was gargling. Bright specks of blood sprayed on to his lips.

He sank back on his haunches, his eyes rolling upwards in their sockets.

The figure stepped into his blurred view.

Carraway tried to speak but couldn't force any words from his ravaged throat. Not even when he saw that the figure was gripping the wood and metal crucifix it had taken from above the bed.

The cross was being brandished like a weapon and Carraway once more tried to speak, but one powerful hand clamped round his throat again, holding him steady. The vicar saw what was about to happen but was powerless to prevent it. He managed to mouth one single word: 'God.'

It did him no good.

The figure drove the crucifix down with unstoppable power, plunging the foot of it into Carraway's right eye, driving it so deep that, after the wood and metal had obliterated the orb, it ripped through into the brain beyond.

The crucifix was pulled free, bringing several ragged slivers of flesh with it. Vitreous fluid from the burst eyeball glistened on the shaft of the cross and stained the silver figure of Christ that adorned it.

Blood poured down the vicar's cheeks and his body began to quiver. As the merciful oblivion of unconsciousness began to wash over him, the figure drove the cross into his left eye too.

It burst like an overripe peach.

Carraway sagged backwards slightly but the figure held him upright and steadied itself for one last blow.

42

'Who found him?'

DS Bishop stood looking down at the body of the Reverend Duncan Carraway, ignoring the other uniformed and plain clothes men who moved carefully around inside the bedroom and out on the landing beyond.

'His cleaner,' DC Hall told his colleague. 'She's being treated for shock at the moment.'

'I'm not surprised,' Bishop murmured, his gaze never leaving the ravaged body of the cleric. 'The cause of death looks self-explanatory, right, George?' The detective glanced briefly to his right where the pathologist was removing something from Carraway's face with a pair of tweezers. He dropped the piece of matter into a clear evidence bag and sealed it.

'Yes, it is,' George Hamblett told the DS. 'As I'm sure you can see.'

Bishop nodded and returned his attention to the corpse.

Carraway was lying on his back, his arms stretched out on either side of him. The DS dropped to his knees and scanned the damage that had been done to the face: the two gouged eye sockets now choked with congealed blood; the red and purple bruises around the throat; and the final outrage.

The wood and metal crucifix had been driven a good three inches into the forehead just below the hairline. It protruded from the skull, dried blood and fragments of pulverised bone sticking to the base.

'Even without the benefit of a post-mortem, I'd be willing to say that the trauma to the head killed him,' Hamblett offered.

'No shit,' breathed Hall, looking at the body, his face pale.

'Something symbolic about it?' Bishop mused. 'Killing a vicar with a cross? Have we got a killer with a sense of irony?' He exhaled deeply. 'What about those?' He pointed to the bruises on Carraway's neck and throat.

'He wasn't killed by strangulation,' Hamblett said. 'My guess is he was still alive when he was stabbed in the eyes. It was that final blow that killed him.'

'I'd like your report as soon as possible, George,' the DS said, getting to his feet. He turned and headed for the landing, followed by Hall.

The two men made their way down the stairs

and out of the house. Despite the breeze that was blowing, it felt humid. The sky was heavy with rain clouds.

Bishop reached for his cigarettes and lit one.

'Let's have a look at the others,' he said, striding across the road in the direction of the cemetery.

There were several police cars and an ambulance parked outside the main entrance to Copsley Fields. Bishop nodded a greeting to a couple of uniformed constables as he made his way into the graveyard. There he stopped for a moment, surveying the large expanse of ground.

It seemed that there were members of the emergency services everywhere, all of them moving about quickly and efficiently as they went about their business.

'Just run through it again, Dan?' Bishop said, gazing around him.

'Nine graves dug up,' Hall began. 'The same ones that were disturbed the other night.' The DC hesitated slightly. 'Seven of the bodies are missing this time.'

Bishop nodded and began walking towards the closest of the desecrated resting places. As he drew nearer, the three policemen round the grave stepped back to allow him better access.

Bishop looked down into the grave. He scrutinised the dark earth that had spilled over the edges of the hole.

'There should be more dirt around the grave,' the

detective muttered. 'If someone was working away with a shovel then why isn't there earth all over the place?'

DC Hall looked quizzically at him.

'And why is the coffin still in there?' Bishop went on.

'The coffins weren't removed from any of the graves, guv,' Hall told him. 'Only the bodies.'

'Don't you think that's strange?' Bishop asked. 'Whoever dug them up climbed down into the grave, opened the box and removed the body. Then, afterwards, he filled the hole in again. It doesn't make sense. It would have taken too long. What do you reckon to dig each one up? Half an hour? Longer? Then another twenty minutes to fill them in again. That's close to an hour for each grave. Nine hours in total. That's a long time. And if the motive was desecration then why fill the fucking things in again?'

Hall could only shake his head.

Bishop turned and headed towards one of the other disturbed graves. The coffin had been pulled clear by two forensics men who were dusting it for fingerprints.

'That's another thing that's weird,' Bishop said, gazing at the casket. 'It doesn't look as if the lid's been prised open. There are no marks on the wood. Unscrewing them would have taken time, too.'

'So how did he get the bodies out?' Hall wondered.

'And then, after he'd removed them from the coffins, he'd have to get them out of the cemetery itself. And all without anyone noticing.'

'I'd say it's impossible, but obviously it's not because some bastard's managed it.'

'Any ideas, boys?' Bishop said, looking at the two forensics men.

'You were right about the lids not having been prised off,' said one of them. He allowed the words to trail away, dropping his gaze as well.

'And?' Bishop insisted, seeing the look on the man's face.

Taking the lid of the coffin in his gloved hands, the man lifted it from the casket.

'The silk on the inside of the lid is torn in a couple of places,' he said, indicating the damage to the sleek material. 'And there are scratches on the wood too. It's the same with the other coffins.'

'What are you telling me?' Bishop asked, his voice low.

The forensics man cleared his throat, looked at his companion briefly, as if for support, and then continued speaking, albeit a little hesitantly.

'From the state of the boxes – the lack of damage to the wood on the outside and the tearing of the silk in the lids – it looks as if the coffins were pushed open from the *inside*.'

43

'Which we all know is impossible,' Bishop said slowly, his eyes never leaving the forensics man.

'Just as it was impossible for Emmanuel Agassa's body to be removed from the hospital morgue,' DC Hall murmured.

'Thanks, boys,' said Bishop, nodding. 'Come on, Dan.'

The two detectives set off across the cemetery towards an area that was surrounded by white sheets fixed to tall wooden poles. The cordon was fully six feet high, preventing a look at what lay within.

Unfortunately, Bishop knew only too well what it was.

'Opened from the inside,' Hall said as they walked.

'Yeah, I heard what he said, Dan,' the DS replied, his gaze fixed straight ahead. 'How did he get the bodies out of here? Seven bodies removed from their graves. Whoever took them would have to put them in a van or a truck or something. If he carried them out one by one it would have taken even more time.'

'No tyre tracks were found anywhere,' Hall said, gesturing round the cemetery. 'Apart from the murdered girl's shoes, there was nothing. The gates were still locked when we arrived this morning.'

Bishop slowed his pace as he reached the cordon of white sheets. Both he and Hall could hear voices on the other side of the makeshift perimeter. The DS paused a moment, then pulled the sheets open and stepped through.

A police photographer was snapping pictures of the bodies of Gemma Hill and Craig Finn, while a forensics man hovered over Gemma's corpse like a vulture over carrion.

He looked up and nodded a greeting to Bishop, who returned the gesture, his gaze moving between the two bodies.

'Cause of death?' he murmured.

'The girl was strangled,' the forensics man told him, indicating the vivid scratches and indentations on Gemma's throat. 'The bloke had his neck broken.'

'Any sexual interference with either of them?'

Gemma was naked from the waist down, her skirt pushed up to her stomach. Finn's jeans and under-pants were pulled down as far as his knees.

'If there are any semen traces inside her, I'm betting they're his,' the forensics man said, nodding towards Finn. 'Sex wasn't the motive for these murders.'

'Thanks, Sherlock.' Bishop smiled.

'Sorry. Ignore me. I wasn't trying to tell you your job.'

'I know that,' Bishop replied. 'To be honest, we're grateful for any fucking input at the moment.' Close to him, the camera flashbulb exploded once again. 'Can you give me a time of death?'

'Between eleven and eleven thirty,' the forensics man told him.

'About the same time as the vicar,' Hall interjected. 'Same killer?'

'We won't know that until the prints have been analysed but I'd say it was more than likely,' Bishop said. 'He kills these two then nips over the road and does the Reverend Duncan. Or the other way round.'

'And removes seven bodies from their graves and takes them with him?' Hall muttered.

Bishop didn't answer.

'Could he have killed them because they saw him digging the bodies up?' the forensics man wanted to know.

'I doubt it,' Hall answered. 'Not from the positions and states of these corpses.'

'With these two,' Bishop said quietly, 'he must have killed the bloke first. Taken him by surprise. Broken his neck then strangled the girl before she could run. If they were having sex then it's not out of the question they didn't hear him sneaking up on them. That's more feasible than that they disturbed him while he was robbing the graves.'

'Why kill the vicar?' Hall enquired.

'Your guess is as good as mine, Dan.'

Bishop pulled the sheet aside, took one last look at the two bodies lying before him, then walked away. Hall hurried after him.

'Three murders and seven bodies stolen in one night,' the DS muttered. 'What the fuck is going on?'

'What do we do next?' Hall asked.

'Wait for the coroner's and forensic reports. See if they give us anything else to go on. Any clues to a suspect.'

'At least these three didn't have those marks on them,' Hall offered. 'The cross-shaped wounds we found on Agassa and the corpses that were dug up.'

'I just hope to God that doesn't mean we've got two nutters on the loose.'

'Who the hell would steal corpses, guv? What kind of sicko does that?'

'There's got to be a reason. Something we don't understand. Something we haven't discovered yet.'

'A religious thing? You said you thought the killing of the vicar might be symbolic.'

'I don't know, Dan.'

Bishop reached into his jacket pocket and pulled out his mobile.

'Make sure the cemetery's closed until further notice,' he said to Hall. 'No one comes in until I say so. You go back to the station and wait for the media. Once this gets out they'll want information. Tell them a statement will be issued in due course. Stall them if you have to.'

Hall nodded and hurried away from his superior.

Bishop waited a moment then flipped open his phone. With his free hand he felt in his pocket for Pearson's card.

The call was answered almost immediately.

'Pearson, it's Bishop,' the detective said. 'We need to talk. It's urgent.'

44

As he brought the Audi to a halt next to the police cars parked outside the Copsley Fields cemetery, Nick Pearson could see several uniformed constables standing around the gates. One was talking animatedly to a man in his seventies who was gesturing towards the graveyard. The older man, Pearson noted, had a bunch of cellophane-wrapped flowers in his hand.

The journalist was about to swing himself out of his car when he saw a familiar figure heading in his direction.

DS Bishop held up a hand both in greeting and to signal that Pearson should stay in his car.

Pearson nodded and sat waiting as the detective slumped heavily into the passenger seat of the Audi.

'What's going on?' the newsman asked.

'I wish I knew,' Bishop said, trying to force a smile.

'What *do* you know?'

'That three people were murdered last night. Two of them inside the cemetery. The other one was the vicar, Duncan Carraway. Nine graves were disturbed and seven bodies were stolen. We haven't got a clue where they are, who took them or why.' The detective shrugged. 'There you go. Now you know as much as I do.'

'Jesus,' Pearson breathed.

'The cemetery's closed until our investigations are completed. That could take a while.'

'Which graves were robbed?' Pearson wanted to know.

'The same graves that were disturbed the other night were tampered with again. It's just that seven bodies were actually taken away this time. Christ knows why.'

The two men sat silently in the car for a moment.

'Did you have any luck identifying those marks we found on the stolen bodies?' Bishop asked at last.

'They were the same as the ones I saw on the corpses in Liberia, but what they mean . . .' He shrugged and allowed the sentence to tail off. 'Did you find anything out from the Africans you interviewed?'

'Nothing. All I did find out was that they seem to have found themselves a spokesman,' Bishop said, smiling thinly. 'A guy who lives at the Western Road flats. We bumped into him when we were taking statements. He speaks good English. He was pretty helpful.'

194

'What was his name?'

'Monde. Mowini. Something like that,' Bishop said, struggling to recall the name. 'Mowende, that was it. Mowende.'

Pearson turned his head sharply to look at the detective.

'Victor Mowende?' he asked.

'Yeah.'

'Tall guy, big built? Looks like he's half asleep?'

Bishop nodded.

'Mowende's living in Darworth?' Pearson demanded.

'Who the hell is he? How do you know him?'

'He was a politician. Or at least that was what he called himself. He wasn't much more than a terrorist, to be honest. He fought in half a dozen of the civil wars in Africa during the last ten years. He was imprisoned about a year ago. I heard the other day that he'd escaped.'

'It seems strange he'd risk turning up here using his own name. He never showed up on our system. Why was he imprisoned in the first place?'

'It's a long story,' Pearson said.

'I need to know what you know about this guy. And as soon as possible.'

'Meet me at my hotel, eight o'clock tonight.'

Bishop nodded and swung himself out of the Audi. He was about to walk away when a uniformed man hurried up to him.

'Excuse me, sir,' he said. 'Someone wants to speak

to you. He's demanding entry to the cemetery. He won't leave.'

'You told him no one was allowed in?' Bishop said.

'Yes, sir, but he's not having it.'

'All right, I'll talk to him. What's his name?'

'Stephen Kirkland.'

Pearson was barely five minutes away from the cemetery when his mobile phone rang.

He reached for it, guiding the car out of traffic and into a deserted side street as he flipped it open.

He didn't recognise the number.

'Hello,' he said, glancing at the neat rows of houses on either side of the narrow road.

'Nick Pearson?'

'Yes. Who's that?'

'My name is Emily Juma.'

Pearson searched his memory.

'We talked the other day at the Western Road flats,' the voice continued.

'I remember. I'm sorry, I couldn't place the name for a second. You kept my card, then?'

'I must meet you as soon as possible. It's my daughter, Wanza. She is missing. You must help me.'

'Have you called the police?'

'I need your help. They do not care, I told you that. Help me find her.'

'Tell me where to meet you. Shall I come to your flat?'

'No.' There was what sounded like panic in the word. 'No. You must not come to my home.'

'All right. Listen, Emily,' Pearson said, aware of the anguish in the woman's voice. 'When I drove to the flats the other day I passed some shops not far away.'

'I know them.'

'There was a café there. Meet me in that café at three o'clock. Can you do that?'

'Yes. Please help me,' she blurted, then the line went dead.

Pearson looked at the phone for a second then slid it back into his pocket. He glanced at the dashboard clock.

It was two twenty-six p.m.

45

The insectocutor behind the counter crackled as a wasp flew into its glowing blue bars. Nick Pearson turned briefly in the direction of the sound then returned to his mug of lukewarm tea.

There were only three other people in the café. Two women in their seventies were chatting contentedly and a lad in his teens was poring over the local paper, occasionally scribbling something in the margins with the biro he was using.

Outside, Pearson could see people going about their business. The small parade of shops on the Walden Hills estate provided for the needs of most. There were men's and women's hairdressers. A launderette. A DIY store, a supermarket, a newsagent's (complete with small post office inside) and a bakery as well as the café in which he now sat. About a hundred yards up the road was a small petrol station, and in the other direction he had seen a Chinese takeaway and a fish and chip shop.

Pearson glanced at his watch then out of the window once more.

It was three seventeen p.m.

He was beginning to wonder where Emily Juma had got to.

Pearson finished what was left in his mug and got to his feet, wandering over to the counter where he ordered another. He watched as the rotund woman in the blue smock refilled the mug from the huge stainless steel urn at the end of the counter. Pearson paid and returned to his seat.

Outside, he heard the sound of a barking dog. It was followed by some unintelligible shouting, both noises eclipsed as a motorbike roared past.

A black woman cautiously approached the door of the café. Pearson recognised her immediately as Emily Juma.

The two old women also glanced briefly at the newcomer then returned to their conversation. The young lad continued scribbling away on his newspaper.

Emily Juma pushed open the café door and walked in.

Pearson got to his feet. 'Emily,' he said, beckoning the woman towards him.

The woman nodded, looking anxiously at the other occupants of the café, and stepped back outside. Pearson followed, watched by the two old women. He caught up with Emily just outside the door.

'We can't talk here,' she said, looking round nervously. 'He will see.'

'Who'll see?'

Two boys of fourteen hurtled past on pushbikes, their school blazers flapping in the breeze.

'Black bitch,' one shouted as they sped by. The other laughed mockingly.

'My car's parked over there,' Pearson said, pointing towards the row of stationary vehicles outside the supermarket. 'We can talk in there if you feel more comfortable.'

Emily nodded and turned towards the cars, casting a wary glance around her again before following him.

The journalist unlocked the Audi and let Emily climb in before he slid behind the steering wheel and started the engine.

'Shall we drive while we're talking?' he said cheerfully.

Emily Juma nodded.

Pearson pulled out into the road and drove off slowly.

'Who do you think is watching you, Emily?' he wanted to know. 'Your husband? The father of your child?'

'Please help me find my daughter,' Emily Juma said pitifully.

'Where did she disappear from?' Pearson asked. 'From your home? From school?'

'She was playing outside. She didn't come in when

200

I called her,' Emily said, wiping her eyes. 'Two days she's been gone.'

'Why did you wait two days to tell me about this? And the police might have been able to help you.'

'I was afraid,' Emily admitted. She fumbled in the pocket of her jeans and pulled out a small photo, which she pushed towards Pearson. 'This is my daughter.'

'She's a beautiful little girl,' he said, glancing at the picture. 'Can I keep this? Just for now?'

Emily nodded. 'She isn't the first child to go missing since he arrived,' she said.

'How many others are missing?'

'Two. Another girl and a boy. The girl is eight years old. The boy is ten.'

'And how long have they been missing?'

'More than a day.'

'You said they'd been missing since he arrived,' Pearson persisted. 'Who is he?'

There was a long silence.

'Is it the same man you're frightened might be watching you?'

Emily nodded. 'His name is Victor Mowende,' she breathed.

46

'What makes you think this man is responsible for the children's disappearance?' Pearson asked.

Emily Juma didn't speak.

'If you want me to help you find your daughter, Emily, then you'll have to tell me everything you know.'

'Mowende came here and the children were gone.'

'Is he staying in the Western Road flats?'

Emily nodded.

'Then you have to tell the police,' Pearson said. 'If you think he's to blame for your daughter and the other two children going missing you must tell them.'

'He came here not long ago,' Emily said. 'Many are afraid of him.'

'What about the parents of the other missing children? Is that why they haven't come forward? Because they're afraid of Mowende?'

Emily nodded.

'Why are you so sure he's to blame?'

'You must help us,' the African woman said. 'You. Not the police.'

'Why me? Why don't you want the police involved?'

'We don't want to make trouble. People hate us anyway. I told you that.'

'The police don't hate you. They're here to protect everyone.'

'They cannot protect us against Mowende. Not if he finds out we have spoken to anyone about the children.'

'If I'm going to help you then I have to know everything,' Pearson told her. 'What are the names of the other two missing children?'

'Daniel Edusi and Anne Omondi.'

'And do their parents know that you're speaking to me?'

'They would not come forward. They are too afraid.'

'Of Mowende?'

'They think their children will come back to them,' Emily said. 'But they will not. Not if Mowende has them.'

'So you think he's holding them captive some- where? Why would he be doing that?'

Emily wiped tears from her cheeks. 'Find my daughter,' she said imploringly.

Pearson saw that the African woman was shaking uncontrollably.

'I'll do everything I can, Emily,' he assured her. 'I promise you.' He drove in silence for a moment or two.

'Let me out now,' Emily Juma said finally.

'I can take you back.'

'No. No one must see me speaking to you.'

Pearson swung the car into the side of the road and brought it to a halt. The African woman clambered out.

'You can ring me any time you need to,' Pearson said. 'Is there some way I can contact you if I have to?'

Emily shook her head. 'I will come to you when I must,' she said, wiping tears from her cheeks.

Pearson watched the African woman walk away. Then he pulled slowly out into the traffic once again.

He glanced down at the picture of Wanza Juma lying on the passenger seat.

47

'We're hitting brick walls,' DS Bishop grunted. 'No motives. No suspects. Nothing. And, on top of that, I've got Stephen Kirkland throwing his weight around. Demanding that I reopen the cemetery so he can visit his brother's grave. I didn't think it was wise, at the moment, to tell him that the poor bastard's body's been removed from it and stolen. I've got enough with murder and grave robbing without trying to handle a riot as well.' The detective ran a hand through his hair and sighed.

Pearson, silhouetted against the window of his hotel room, sipped at the vodka and lemonade he was holding.

'Are you sure you won't join me?' he asked. 'You sound as if you need something stronger than orange juice.'

Bishop merely shook his head and rolled his glass between his palms.

'What did you tell Kirkland?' Pearson asked.

'Same as all the others,' Bishop said. 'That there were two murders in the cemetery last night and we need time to go over the place for forensic evidence.'

'But Kirkland wasn't going for that?'

'He didn't have any choice.' Bishop sighed. 'But he wasn't happy.'

'How long can you keep the cemetery shut down?'

'As long as I need to.'

Pearson nodded. 'It might take longer than you think when you hear what I've got to say,' he said. 'Not only is Victor Mowende here in Darworth, he's the one Emily Juma thinks has taken the children.'

Bishop held up a hand. 'Hang on a minute,' he said. '"Taken the children"? What children?'

'Three children have supposedly gone missing from the Western Road flats in the last three days,' Pearson explained. 'The mother of one of them contacted me and said she thought that Victor Mowende could be responsible.'

'Why the hell didn't you tell me?' Bishop exclaimed.

'I only found out this afternoon,' Pearson said. 'And it hasn't been confirmed that they're actually missing yet.'

Bishop nodded. 'I'd better get someone on it,' he said, reaching for his mobile.

'I said I'd help her,' Pearson interrupted. 'She doesn't want the police involved. Let me handle it. We don't know if it's a criminal matter yet anyway.'

Bishop hesitated.

'Let me find out if the kids are even missing before your guys go blundering in there,' Pearson continued. 'I think she trusts me.'

'Why you?'

Pearson shrugged. 'She must have her reasons.'

'And this woman thinks that Mowende's responsible?' the detective murmured. 'Why?'

'She's terrified of him. By the sound of it, they all are up at those flats. And I think they might have good reason to be.'

Bishop turned to look at the journalist.

'I did some more research on him,' Pearson continued. 'I rang a couple of journalist friends – foreign correspondents who've worked in Africa, as I did. Mowende was more powerful than you can imagine.' He opened his laptop and brought up some text and two photographs. 'Mowende was born in Liberia. Details are sketchy about his early life, even exactly how old he is. But he had a fairly decent education because he ended up as an aide to some government minister and then, when that guy was murdered, as a captain in the Liberian army. It might not surprise you to find out that Mowende himself was one of the main suspects in the murder.' Pearson clicked on one of the images of Mowende and enlarged it. 'As I told you before, he fought in half a dozen civil and inter-tribal wars during the late nineties. He sort of disappeared off the radar about five years ago but when he stuck his head up again, it was as a politician.' Pearson scrolled down to another photo of Mowende and two other black men. All three were dressed in suits and had their arms round each other. 'You might recognise the guy on the right. Robert Mugabe. The president of Zimbabwe. He was rumoured to be supplying arms to Mowende's faction in Sierra Leone.'

'Who's the other bloke?'

'That's the former head of the Liberian Secret Police. Also thought to have been murdered by Mowende and his followers.'

'Followers?' Bishop interjected. 'You make him sound like some kind of cult leader.'

'Pretty close,' Pearson told him. 'Mowende tried to engineer a coup against the government of Sierra Leone. If it'd worked, he planned to install himself as president. That's one of the reasons he had to get out of there. He was chased out by his enemies when the coup failed. That's why he's here in this country.'

'But if Mowende was a politician, a powerful man, why the hell is he living in some crappy old council flats here in Darworth?' Bishop wanted to know. 'Why didn't he just claim political asylum and use his money to live in a penthouse somewhere?'

'Because politics wasn't the only reason he left Africa. He had to get out as quickly as possible.

Before he could get his hands on the money he'd accumulated over the past few years. He ran with the clothes he had on his back and the money he had in his pockets.'

'Why did he have to get away so quickly? Because the coup failed?'

'That was one reason,' Pearson said flatly. 'The other was because he was wanted for murder.'

'You implied he might have killed any number of people over the years,' Bishop reminded him. 'Why did he run this time?'

'Because he had a death sentence hanging over him,' Pearson told him. 'He'd already been arrested, tried and sentenced. He was snatched from prison by some of his followers. But the murders he'd been convicted of weren't political or military. They were ritual killings. He murdered six children and at least four women. He'd been found guilty of practising Uthalande.'

Bishop looked in bewilderment at the journalist.

'To you and me?' Pearson said. 'Voodoo.'

48

Bishop looked quizzically at the journalist.

'Voodoo?' the DS said and the word seemed to reverberate around the room. Even speaking it felt strange to the detective.

'Uthalande,' Pearson said again. 'It's one of the many kinds of tribal magic. In Africa it's looked on as a religion. It believes that everything on earth is controlled by the spirits of the dead. So, its followers communicate with the spirits in order to control their own fate.' Pearson saw the look on Bishop's face. 'I know it sounds crazy but I'm only telling you what I found out.'

'Go on,' the detective urged.

'It allows the worshipper to create his own destiny using either white or black magic. It makes no distinction between the two. What is interesting is that the main worship and practice of Uthalande is carried out around something called a *nganga*, a sacrificial cauldron. Do you know what they put in that cauldron? The contents of desecrated graves.'

'Jesus,' Bishop murmured.

'The ritual also includes human sacrifice,' Pearson continued. 'Usually women and children.'

Bishop swallowed hard.

'And there's something else,' Pearson went on. 'Followers have been known to carve symbols into their flesh and also into the flesh of their victims. When those marks are made in the flesh of the dead, it supposedly allows the person who did it to control them. Raise them from the dead.'

'So you're trying to tell me that Mowende's some kind of fucking witch doctor?' Bishop said.

'I'm just telling you what I found out,' the journalist repeated. 'The fact is a lot of this stuff ties in with what's been happening here in Darworth. Mowende arrives and straight away you've got graves being disturbed, bodies being taken. Bodies with symbols carved into them. Now some kids have gone missing and the people who live around Mowende are scared of him. Perhaps that's because they know who he is. The kind of power he has.'

'Raising the dead?' the detective said quietly. 'I thought you were supposed to be the hard-bitten cynical journalist, Pearson. Are you telling me you believe this shit?'

'You can be sure the people who live around

Mowende do,' Pearson retaliated. 'The power of suggestion can be very potent.'

The policeman took a sip from his glass.

'A follower of Uthalande would need those kids to help him maintain his power,' Pearson said.

Bishop shook his head. 'I can't believe that,' he said. 'Tribal magic? Human sacrifice? Controlling the dead? This is real life, Pearson, not a fucking horror movie. We're in Darworth, not Haiti. You'll be telling me next Mowende's got some kind of zombie army waiting to attack us.'

'They don't call them zombies,' said Pearson flatly. 'They call them servants.'

'And I suppose they shuffle around like cripples and eat human brains. Just like in the films.' Bishop snorted.

'Followers of Uthalande believe that the reanimated bodies look and behave exactly the way they did when they died,' Pearson corrected him. 'Reanimating the corpse can even stop or reverse the process of decomposition. The only difference is, they're under the control of the person who summoned them back from the dead.'

'Christ almighty.' Bishop gaped. 'And people actually believe this?'

'That a man could die and be resurrected? That's the basis of the Christian religion. Why not?'

'Very clever, Pearson,' snapped Bishop. 'But you're not talking about Jesus. You're talking about someone who can bring people back from the dead.'

'If you believe the Bible, Christ himself raised

Lazarus from the dead,' the journalist pointed out. 'Where's the difference?'

'Let me get this straight,' the detective muttered. 'You're telling me that Mowende has the power to raise the dead and that's where the missing bodies have gone?'

'I didn't say that,' Pearson said, shaking his head. 'I told you what I know about Mowende and his beliefs.'

'All right, tell me what you do think.'

'The information about his religion is right,' Pearson said defiantly. 'They use bones and bodies from graves. Mowende's got to be a suspect, hasn't he? As for the missing kids, I don't know.'

'If it's a religion then there could be others up at the Western Road flats who are helping him,' Bishop said. 'But you said yourself that they were frightened of him. Why help him?'

'They're probably helping him *because* they're scared of him.'

'I'm going to have to question him again,' Bishop said.

'On what charge?' Pearson wanted to know. 'Suspicion of practising his religion?'

'If his religion involves grave robbing and ritual murder then yes,' the detective snapped. 'The missing bodies belong to residents of this town.'

'But if they were black it wouldn't be as important?'

'Oh, come on,' the DS said wearily. 'This isn't a racial issue.'

'It will be if Stephen Kirkland and his little gang find out about this.'

'They won't find out,' Bishop assured him. He exhaled deeply. 'We're talking about murder. Besides, the body of Emmanuel Agassa is also missing, remember? This affects the Africans as well as everyone else.'

'But Agassa's body disappeared before Mowende got here,' Pearson said.

'We don't know the exact date of Mowende's arrival in Darworth,' the detective countered. 'We can't say for sure. As it stands, he's the number one suspect.'

Bishop's mobile phone rang. He checked the caller number.

'I've got to take this,' he said.

Pearson nodded and turned to look out of the hotel window. Outside, the sodium glare of street lights cast long shadows. He watched people walking past unconcernedly. Behind him, Bishop reacted to what was being said with single syllable responses.

When he heard the detective close his phone, Pearson turned back to face him. Bishop looked a little pale.

'That was the pathologist,' he said quietly. 'He apologised for taking so long with the reports on the three murder victims that were found this morning. Apparently he had trouble identifying some of the skin fragments that were left on the bodies.'

Pearson looked at the detective in bewilderment.

'The vicar, the girl and the bloke were all killed the way he first thought,' Bishop continued. 'But the fingerprints on each body were different. He thinks three different people committed the murders.'

'Oh, Christ,' Pearson muttered.

'It gets better,' Bishop continued, smiling humour-lessly. 'The skin fragments left by the killers on the victims were decomposing. He said they looked as if they belonged to people who'd already been dead for more than six months.'

49

For what seemed like an eternity neither man spoke. Then Pearson broke the silence.

'Could he be mistaken?'

'He could, but I doubt it,' Bishop answered. 'He's been doing the job for years. He's no fool.' He sighed. 'So, what does that leave me with? All evidence points to the fact that three people have been murdered by walking corpses?' He shook his head. 'That's going to look great in my fucking report, isn't it?'

'How many graves did you say were disturbed? Nine, wasn't it?' Pearson asked.

'Nine disturbed but the bodies were only removed from seven.'

'What about the other two? What happened to the remains?'

'They were reburied.'

'Why were the bodies left in those two graves?'

'One of them was decapitated, the other was cut up,' said Bishop. 'The arms and legs were removed.'

'So if they were under the control of an Uthalande priest, they couldn't have freed themselves from their coffins anyway,' Pearson said.

Bishop looked vague.

'The seven graves that were found empty,' the journalist went on. 'They were all previously occupied by complete, *whole*, bodies. If we assume for a second that the person who's controlling them—'

'For Christ's sake,' Bishop interrupted. 'This is bullshit.'

'Just hear me out,' Pearson snapped. 'If the bodies were in the power of an Uthalande priest they would have been able to escape from their coffins. You said the lids had been pushed open from the inside, right? Obviously, the two that were mutilated wouldn't have been capable of getting out because of the damage that was done to them the first time the graves were interfered with.'

The detective looked unblinkingly at Pearson, unable or unwilling to speak.

'You've considered *logical* explanations for what's happened,' the journalist continued. 'Try suspending disbelief for a minute. Everything I've ever believed in tells me it's bullshit but we might just be in the middle of something that none of us understand. Something so far out of our experience we can't ever hope to come to terms with it. But because we don't understand it doesn't mean it isn't happening.'

'I don't know what the fuck you're talking about, Pearson. Zombies. Reanimated corpses killing people. Tribal magic.' The detective shook his head.

'There's only one thing left for you to do,' Pearson told him. 'The key might be those other two graves. The ones that still have remains in them.'

'Go on then,' said Bishop challengingly. 'What do I do?'

'Dig them up,' Pearson said flatly. 'Get the pathologist to examine the remains in those two graves. He might find something that explains what happened to the missing corpses. You can override procedures in emergencies, can't you?'

Bishop eyed him warily for a moment then reached for his mobile phone and dialled a number.

'Dan, it's me. I want four men sent to the cemetery now,' he said. 'Tell them to disinter the other two coffins. Yes. Dig them up. I'll meet you there in half an hour.'

Pearson met his gaze and nodded, his face set in hard lines.

50

Pearson and Bishop barely spoke during the drive to the cemetery. The detective was focused on guiding the car and Pearson contented himself with gazing out of the windscreen. Besides, he reasoned, what else was there to say?

There were no words to describe the situation they found themselves in. Not in a sane world.

As Bishop brought the Astra to a halt outside the main gates of Copsley Fields, Pearson felt his heart thudding a little faster.

Anticipation? Excitement? Fear?

They stepped out of the vehicle and the journalist shivered involuntarily. He told himself it was because of the cold breeze that had come with the arrival of night. Above them, the dark sky was filled with banks of scudding clouds that gathered ominously above the cemetery.

Bishop reached into the glove compartment of

the car, pulled out two torches and handed one to Pearson. He flicked it on, playing the powerful beam across the ground ahead of him for a moment before switching it off again.

The two men walked past the police cars parked outside the gates and on into the cemetery itself. Trees near the pathway swayed gently as the wind grew stronger, whistling through the branches to create a discordant accompaniment.

Up ahead Pearson could see movement. Other torch beams occasionally lanced through the darkness. The sound of shovels in earth was clearly audible.

'Should I be here?' he asked, seeing the men toiling away to shift the soil. 'I mean, it is a police matter, isn't it?'

'You're as much a part of this investigation as the rest of us now,' Bishop told him. 'If it wasn't for you, *none* of us would be here now.'

Pearson saw a man slightly younger than himself heading towards them.

'How's it going, Dan?' Bishop asked.

'We've almost uncovered the first coffin,' DC Hall told his superior. He looked questioningly at Pearson.

'This is Nick Pearson,' Bishop said. 'He's helping me with the investigation. He's got specialised knowledge about certain aspects of this case.'

Hall nodded and extended his right hand. Pearson shook it, feeling the strength in the man's grip.

The three of them walked across the wet grass

towards the first of the graves, where two men were busily removing earth. It was piled up high on two sides of the hole.

Pearson flicked on his torch and shone the beam over the headstone.

'Sheila Johnson,' he murmured. 'Died five years ago. She was only twenty-six.'

'Cancer,' Hall murmured.

'She was the who was decapitated,' Bishop said.

'What about the other grave?' the journalist asked. 'Who was buried there?'

'A young lad,' Hall said. 'James Breen. He died about a year ago. Meningitis. He was eight.'

'And he was the one who was cut up?' Pearson enquired.

Hall nodded.

'We'll bring him up after we have a look at this one,' Bishop said.

Pearson stood on the edge of the grave and glanced down. Two more policemen were working in the deep hole, hurling earth out of the black hollow. He heard the unmistakable sound of metal on wood.

'They've reached the coffin,' he said quietly.

The wind blew strongly for a moment, sweeping across the cemetery and once again causing Pearson to shudder. He could still feel his heart beating.

Two long lengths of rope were dropped into the open grave and Pearson watched as they were slipped under the coffin. The two men who had been down in the hole then clambered up and out, one of them brushing dirt from his hands.

Pearson saw each of the four men then take hold of one of the rope ends.

'Bring it up,' Bishop instructed. 'Carefully.'

The men pulled and, as Pearson watched, the coffin slowly rose into view, suspended on the ropes as if it was in some kind of makeshift hammock.

DC Hall guided it to the graveside, putting one hand on the casket to ensure it was set down evenly.

Pearson could see the damage round the lid and one side of the box where the wood had been splintered. He assumed it had been done when the coffin was first disturbed.

'While we have a look in here,' Bishop said, 'start on the other grave.'

The four policemen, shovels in hand, moved away in the direction of James Breen's resting place.

Bishop moved closer to the box and took a screwdriver from Hall, who kept the second for himself, sliding it into position and holding it there. The DS looked at Hall and the younger man nodded.

Pearson took a step closer, his torch aimed at the casket.

'All right,' Bishop breathed, preparing to turn the first of the screws. 'Let's get it open.'

51

Pearson held the torch steady over the coffin as the two detectives carefully loosened the first two screws.

They came free with relative ease from both sides of the lid. Bishop freed the next one on his side with a little more difficulty. Hall, meanwhile, was forced to exert considerable force to remove the second one on his side of the casket. His screwdriver slipped, gouging into the wood. He cursed under his breath, pushed his glasses back up his nose and continued.

As he stood watching, Pearson could hear a faint crackling sound. It took him a moment to realise that it was the wind stirring the cellophane-wrapped bunches of flowers on the adjacent grave. He glanced round in the gloom then returned his attention to the two detectives kneeling in front of him.

'Last one,' Bishop grunted, removing the final screw on his side of the coffin.

A second later Hall did the same.

Both men straightened up.

Pearson was gazing at the casket with the kind of concentration a mongoose reserves for a cobra.

Bishop dropped down once more and hooked his fingers under the rim of the lid, preparing to lift it free.

'Hold that torch steady, Nick,' he said.

He pulled, but the lid wouldn't budge.

'The wood must have expanded,' Pearson offered, still staring at the coffin.

Bishop tried again, and this time the lid came free. The DS placed it on one of the mounds of earth and looked down into the coffin.

Pearson shone the light inside the box.

The beam illuminated the corpse of Sheila Johnson. She had been buried dressed in a charcoal grey skirt and jacket with a white blouse underneath. Pearson noticed that there were muddy stains on the material but his gaze moved swiftly to her severed head. It was propped up on its stump, the hair hanging limply against the sunken cheeks.

'She's been dead for five years,' DC Hall murmured. 'Why isn't there more decomposition?'

Pearson and Bishop glanced swiftly at each other but neither felt inclined to offer a possible explanation.

Bishop knelt beside the coffin and slowly extended his hands towards the head.

'The marks will be on the back of the neck,' Pearson said quietly.

Bishop lifted the head in both hands until he was gazing at the face, his face drawn to the closed eyes.

'The skin feels waxy,' he murmured. 'Pliable.'

He continued looking at the head, inspecting every inch of it with his inquisitive stare.

Pearson aimed the torch beam fully into the woman's face, the light making the pale skin look even whiter. Slowly, the detective turned the head until the beam picked out the now familiar wounds that had been cut into the base of the skull.

Bishop felt something wet drip on to his hand.

Pearson opened his mouth to say something, his eyes fixed on the wounds on the severed head.

Dark liquid was welling up in the gashes.

'The cuts are bleeding,' the journalist breathed, noticing the dark droplet that had fallen on to the skin of the detective.

'That's impossible,' Hall said. 'How can they . . .' The words faded away.

A piercing scream sliced through the air.

It took the men some seconds to realise it had come from the head.

Bishop dropped it and quickly stepped back, looking down at it as it rolled over in the coffin. The mouth was still open, still screaming. Pearson had it fixed in the beam of the torch.

Hall stumbled backwards, mouthing words and shaking all over. Pearson kept his disbelieving gaze fixed on the head, the torch he held now wavering in his grip.

The eyes snapped open.

Pearson found himself staring straight into them as they bulged in their dead sockets.

He was only vaguely aware of movement next to him. Of Bishop reaching for the coffin lid.

The head continued to scream.

Bishop slammed the lid down on to the casket, muffling the horrendous sound, then he shoved the box towards the yawning grave with one foot, desperate to push it back into the hole from which it had been pulled.

'No,' Pearson snapped, pushing the detective aside.

'What the fuck *is* that?' panted DC Hall, gazing with staring eyes at the coffin, the sound of the muffled screams still ringing in his ears.

The men who had been at the other grave had hurried to join them, alerted by the strident shrieks and the commotion.

'What's happening?' one of them asked frantically, hearing the screams.

'She's alive,' Hall blurted, breathlessly, pointing at the coffin. 'She's alive.'

'No she isn't,' Pearson said flatly. He reached for the coffin lid and tore it free, exposing the severed head.

He saw its bloodshot eyes turn in his direction, fixing him in a hateful stare. Blood was still pumping from the cuts at the back of the head and more of the thick fluid had also begun to ooze from the severed veins dangling like bloated worms from the stump of the neck.

The others watched in stunned disbelief. One of the men turned away and vomited.

And, all the time, the head of Sheila Johnson continued to scream.

Pearson snatched a shovel from one of the paralysed policemen and, without hesitation, he struck. He brought the implement down with all his strength on to the skull.

The impact was powerful enough to split the bone. The blade of the shovel shattered the cranium and drove down into the brain beneath.

The screaming degenerated into what sounded like cries of pain. They were almost pitiful. Like the helpless whimperings of a dying puppy.

Pearson found the sound even more unbearable than the screams and he struck again at the head, shearing off another chunk of bone and exposing the brain.

Jellied pieces of greyish-pink matter splattered the silk inside the coffin.

The screaming stopped.

Pearson held the shovel before him, glaring at the head, ready to strike again if he had to. Bishop took a step forward, raising a shaking hand to halt him, while the other men looked on in horrified disbelief.

Bishop leaned closer to the coffin.

'Don't touch it,' Pearson snapped, seeing that the detective was extending a hand towards the severed head once more. He pushed the shovel towards the DS, who took it from him and tentatively prodded the head.

'What's going on?' Hall gasped, staring first at Bishop and then at Pearson.

'We've got to look in that other grave,' Pearson said, choosing to ignore the question.

'What if it's the same?' Bishop asked, still gazing down at the remains before him.

'Then we'll deal with it,' Pearson insisted. 'But we've got to find out.'

'Open the other grave,' the DS said, pushing his way through the men around him.

They hesitated, looking from the coffin of Sheila Johnson to their superior and back again.

'Come on,' Bishop called as he and Pearson trudged across to their next objective.

Neither man spoke. Neither had the words.

52

Nick Pearson cupped his hand around the lighter, shielding the flame from the cold wind that whipped across the cemetery. He lit his cigarette, drew hard on it and looked into the coffin that lay by the graveside.

The body of James Breen, his arms severed at the shoulders and his legs crudely hacked off just above the knees, lay motionless in its small coffin.

Pearson glanced at his watch and noted the time.

'It's almost an hour since we brought this body up,' he said, his gaze now fixed once more on the mutilated corpse. 'And no sign of movement.' He dropped the volume of his voice slightly as if even he found it difficult to say the words. 'No evidence of reanimation.'

'It's . . . it's . . .' DC Hall struggled to speak.

'Crazy?' Pearson offered. 'Insane? Beyond belief?'

'Fucking ridiculous,' Bishop interjected.

'It *is* ridiculous and yet we all saw it,' Pearson said. 'All of us.' He gestured around him at the four policemen who were also standing looking at the empty grave and the coffin it had given up.

'But I don't understand how it's possible,' Hall said, pulling the collar of his jacket up round his neck to protect himself from the wind. 'Even though I saw it. I'm still not sure I believe it. And what you told us about this religion . . .' Again his words faded away as he shook his head incredulously.

'Voodoo,' one of the other policemen murmured.

'My missus watches those zombie films,' another offered. 'All that *Night of the Living Dead* shit. That kind of stuff. I used to laugh at her for getting scared by it. Not any more.'

'If the other missing bodies are being controlled by someone, like you said, then where are they now?' Hall wanted to know. He looked questioningly at Pearson.

The journalist could only shrug.

'When we find out who's controlling them, we might have a chance of finding them,' Bishop said.

'So was Emmanuel Agassa one of these things?' Hall continued. 'Is that why his body disappeared from the hospital?'

'Looks like it,' Bishop conceded. 'That's why forensics only found Agassa's fingerprints and footprints leading out of the morgue. Same with the empty coffins we found here. We couldn't figure out how they were pushed open from the inside. Now it looks as if we've got our answer.'

'There's no way you're going to be able to keep this quiet, Bishop,' said Pearson. 'Not after what happened here tonight.'

'What do you suggest I do?' Bishop wanted to know. 'Call a press conference in the morning and let the media know that we've got eight reanimated dead bodies running around? We've *got* to keep this quiet.' He looked round at the other men, studying each face in turn. 'I don't want anyone talking about what they've seen or heard here tonight, got that? You don't tell your mates, you don't tell your wives or girlfriends. You keep it to yourselves.'

'Nobody would believe us anyway,' the third policeman pointed out. 'And I wouldn't blame them.'

'What *do* we say, guv?' Hall wanted to know.

'We are continuing with the investigation,' Bishop told him. 'We get the pathologist to examine these two bodies. We find out as much as we can about the missing African kids. And I'm going to reopen the cemetery tomorrow.'

'Won't forensics want more time to look at the bodies?'

'Fuck forensics,' Bishop said sharply. 'We reopen the cemetery tomorrow.'

'So it was the Africans all along?' the second policeman said. Bishop met the man's gaze and saw something like anger in his eyes. 'Fucking black bastards.'

'Watch your mouth,' Bishop snapped. 'I don't want the racial elements of this case to get out of hand.'

'But it's those bastards who've done this, sir,' the constable said. 'No one else.'

'No one knows that for sure,' Pearson said. 'The fact that Uthalande originated in Africa doesn't make all Africans guilty. That'd be like calling every German a Nazi.'

'Well, you would say that, wouldn't you?' the constable sneered. 'But you were the one who told us about them.'

'I only told you about their beliefs,' Pearson protested.

'Beliefs that have done this,' the policeman hissed, pointing at the mutilated remains of James Breen. 'White people don't believe in fucking voodoo. It must be them. Why are you defending them?'

'Nobody's defending them and nobody's siding with them,' Bishop interrupted.

'He tells us they're to blame and then denies it,' the policeman said, pointing an angry finger at Pearson. 'It's obvious it's them.'

'Nothing about this fucking case is obvious,' Bishop snapped. 'Unfortunately.' He sucked in a deep breath. 'When we're checking on the missing kids we'll ask questions. Discreetly. We can't do anything else. No one said they can't practise their own religion in this country.'

'Well, perhaps someone should,' the constable said irritably. 'We let Muslims practise their own fucking religion and London got bombed.'

Bishop held up his hand to silence him.

For a moment, the only sound that broke the stillness was the high-pitched whine of the wind through the trees.

'So what's the next step, guv?' Hall asked finally.

'Fill these graves in again,' the DS said. 'I don't want anyone who visits the cemetery tomorrow knowing we've been here tonight. And as I said before, no one opens their mouth about any of this. Understand?'

The other men nodded.

Pearson took one last drag on his cigarette then dropped it at his feet. It hissed on the wet grass. He watched as the policemen began shovelling earth back into the open grave of James Breen.

Bishop reached inside his jacket for his mobile and jabbed the digits he wanted. While he waited for it to be answered, Pearson wandered away, towards the coffin of Sheila Johnson. He stood beside it, looking at the body and the severed head within. After a moment he heard footsteps on the gravel path close to him.

'The remains will be picked up and taken to the hospital,' Bishop said. 'The pathologist's going to examine them.'

'Does he know what happened here?'

'I didn't mention it just now on the phone, but when the time comes I'll have to.'

The two men stood by the graveside for a moment longer, both transfixed by the sight before them and

233

still unable to believe what they had seen and experienced earlier that night.

'Rowley's got a point,' the detective said slowly. 'About the Africans being to blame for these desecrations. It all points to them.'

'It doesn't give people like him the right to start kicking their doors down.'

'People like who? White people?'

'You said this wasn't a racial thing.'

'All right then, the people whose loved ones have had their graves desecrated. People like Stephen Kirkland. What am I supposed to tell him if he finds out his brother's body is missing?'

Pearson had no answer.

'When I said no one opens their mouth about this, I meant you too,' Bishop said quietly.

'What's that supposed to mean?' Pearson demanded, looking at the detective.

'You're still a journalist and this is one hell of a story. You came to Darworth to do a story, didn't you?'

'Give me some credit, Bishop. What would be the point? Who the fuck would believe *this*?'

53

It was almost eleven a.m. when Pearson finally woke.

He rolled over in bed, shielding his eyes from the unseasonal sunshine pouring through the hotel bedroom window, and glanced at his watch.

'Shit,' he murmured.

He lay on his back, trying to recover his thoughts. His mind went spinning back to the previous night. To the cemetery. To the opening of the coffins. He could still see the screaming head of Sheila Johnson when he closed his eyes, as if the image had burned itself on to his retina.

He remembered returning to the hotel at Christ knows what time. He recalled not being able to sleep. The thoughts that had clogged his mind last night had prevented that luxury.

He'd finally dropped off at about three a.m. as

far as he could remember, tormented by what he'd seen at the cemetery earlier. But mixed with the horror of the situation was the sheer *(what was the word?)* madness of it all.

Madness? That was right, wasn't it? Appropriate too.

Pearson sat up slowly, gazing straight ahead.

You're involved in something beyond your experience and understanding. Something you yourself would never have believed had you not witnessed it first hand.

The journalist ran a hand through his hair and was about to swing himself out of bed when his mobile rang.

'Hello,' he said, stifling a yawn.

'Mr Pearson, this is Emily Juma. I have to meet you. It is important.'

'Emily,' Pearson said, rubbing his eyes with his free hand.

'I have to meet you,' the voice at the other end of the phone repeated.

'When?'

'Tomorrow at four o'clock. Please don't tell anyone.'

'What's wrong?'

'Tomorrow at four o'clock,' she repeated. 'I have to go now.'

There was a rasp of static.

Dead line.

★　★　★

DS Martin Bishop scanned the report once more.

'So, there were no signs of additional mutilation on the body of James Breen,' he murmured, his eyes still fixed on the report.

'If there had been I'd have mentioned it,' George Hamblett told him.

'And none on the bodies of Gemma Hill, Craig Finn or Duncan Carraway? No marks like the ones on the back of Sheila Johnson's skull?'

Hamblett shook his head.

'So, if the information we've got so far is correct,' Bishop mused, 'there's no way the three murder victims can be reanimated. I suppose I should be grateful for that, at least.'

'Unless there's more than one way of doing it. I mean, we don't know how the process works to begin with so we can't be sure those other three bodies will remain dormant. We'll just have to wait and see. You could post men at the gravesides to check, but apart from that . . .' He shrugged as the words tailed off.

Bishop frowned and looked again at the reports, his heart thudding a little harder against his ribs.

As Emily Juma made her way through the flat she passed by the door to her daughter's room. Emily paused for a moment then turned the handle and looked inside.

The small bed was occupied by two large, battered teddy bears. Emily moved across to the bed and picked up the larger of the two stuffed animals. She could smell her daughter on it.

She gazed at the teddy, seeing herself reflected in its large, sightless eyes for a second, then replaced it and left the room.

54

'Detective Bishop.'

Victor Mowende smiled as he opened the door of his flat, running appraising eyes over the two policemen before him.

'You've got a good memory, Mr Mowende,' the DS told him.

'Your colleague's name, unfortunately, I *don't* remember,' the African said.

'Detective Constable Hall,' the younger detective said, flashing his ID.

'Of course,' Mowende said amiably. He stepped aside and ushered the two men into the flat, then showed them through into the living room. 'Please sit down.' He gestured towards the faded sofa.

The detectives accepted his invitation.

'Mr Mowende, I need to ask you some questions,' Bishop told him, watching as the tall African seated himself opposite on a high-backed chair.

'I am listening,' Mowende said.

'We know who you are,' Bishop told him flatly. 'Why you're in this country. Why you left Sierra Leone. We know that you'd been convicted of murder. That's why you fled. That's why you're here.'

Mowende smiled and steepled his fingers before him.

'So, are you here to arrest me, Detective?' he asked.

'You know I can't do that. Not for a crime you committed in another country when there's no extradition order on you. I checked. You're also registered with the relevent authorities here and in Sierra Leone. You're not an illegal immigrant. You can't be deported.'

'I am lucky to have friends in high places.' Mowende smiled. 'So why are you here?'

'The crimes you were convicted of in Sierra Leone involved ritual aspects,' the detective continued. 'The practice of tribal magic.'

'Uthalande. But if you find the word magic easier then so be it.'

'You admit that you were a practitioner of Uthalande?'

'Of course. It is my religion.'

'A religion that involves the desecration of graves and the raising of dead bodies?'

'We who follow this path do not see it the same way, Detective.'

'But your religion does involve the use of dead bodies,' Bishop said.

Mowende nodded.

'Are there other followers of your religion living in these flats, Mr Mowende?' the DS continued.

'Of course. That would be like me asking you if there are other Christians in this town.'

'So you do still practise your religion?'

'Will you arrest me if I say yes?' Mowende smiled.

'I'll arrest you if I can prove you're responsible for some of the things that have happened.'

'You think that my religion is to blame?'

'Is it?'

'Didn't someone once say that more blood had been spilled in the name of God than anyone else? *Your* god, Detective Bishop. Not mine.' Mowende sneered. 'A white god. Or should I say a god worshipped by the whites. All through history, *your* history, people have been persecuted and slaughtered, killed in their millions during wars, because of your religious beliefs.'

'Our god doesn't ask for human sacrifices.'

'Perhaps he should,' Mowende said, smiling. 'Isn't it better that one person dies instead of thousands?'

'So you'd kill for your religion, Mr Mowende?'

'My religion allows a freedom of choice that yours does not, Detective Bishop. Your god demands blind obedience. You cannot question his word. You cannot disagree with his teachings. If you do, you risk damnation.' Mowende smiled mockingly. 'I can show my devotion to my god any way I wish. If I choose to offer a sacrifice then that is my decision. My god will not think any less of me if I don't.'

'What about children?' Bishop asked. 'Are they suitable sacrifices? We have reason to believe that three children who live in these flats have gone missing during the last week. Do you know anything about that, Mr Mowende?'

'What exactly are you accusing me of, Detective Bishop?' the African asked wearily. 'Am I a murderer, a grave robber or a kidnapper? What is my crime?'

'I didn't say you were guilty of any crime, Mr Mowende,' the DS said. 'I'm just trying to explain to you that we've got something of a situation here in Darworth and, from what we've discovered about you and your beliefs, I think we've got every right to wonder if you're implicated.'

'Implicated in the disappearance of three children? What kind of man do you take me for?'

'You were convicted of murder in Sierra Leone, Mr Mowende,' Bishop reminded him. 'You can understand why we've approached you.'

'These children. What are their names?'

Hall pulled a notebook from his inside pocket and flipped it open.

'Wanza Juma, Anne Omondi and Daniel Edusi,' he read. 'Do you know any of them?'

The African considered the names carefully then shook his head slowly.

'What about their parents?' Bishop said. 'Do you know them?'

242

Again the tall African shook his head.

'Haven't you spoken to anyone else since you arrived here?' Bishop snapped. 'Or is it just a co-incidence you haven't spoken to these people?'

'I like to keep myself to myself, Detective.'

'You wouldn't object to us searching your flat?'

'If you want to search my home, you may.' Mowende gestured expansively around him with one large hand. 'Do it now. You don't need a warrant. I give you my permission.'

'Not at the moment,' Bishop told him. 'But bear in mind you will be receiving further visits from us.'

'Are you threatening me?'

'Warning you, Mr Mowende. There's a difference. At least there is in this country.'

Mowende got to his feet. 'Then if you don't intend to arrest me, perhaps you will leave me now,' he said quietly.

The two detectives also stood, and Hall led the way towards the front door.

'I hope you find the children, Detective Bishop,' Mowende said. 'If there's anything I can do to help, then I will.'

'You said there were other people living here who practised your religion,' Bishop said. 'Can you tell us who?'

'I go from suspect to informer in the space of one conversation,' Mowende said, smiling crookedly. 'I don't know who practises Uthalande. If I did I would tell you, Detective Bishop. If it would spare myself and my people further persecution I would lead you to them now.'

Bishop held the tall African's gaze for a moment.

'Thank you, Mr Mowende,' he said. 'We'll speak again soon.'

The African closed the door gently on the two detectives.

Bishop turned and walked away, Hall close beside him.

'Arrogant bastard,' Bishop hissed.

'Do you think he knows something about the missing kids?'

'We'll keep him under surveillance for a couple of days,' the DS pronounced. 'Question him again. I want him to know he's being watched. I want him sweating.'

55

The kitchen of the house was small, barely ten feet square. Hardly big enough to accommodate the wooden table and four chairs it boasted.

Drips from one of the sink taps fell into the bowl beneath, rippling the dirty water. Plates, saucepans, a grill pan and two frying pans were jammed into the bowl, all of them unwashed. There was congealed grease on two of the worktops and a rusty toaster had spilled crumbs everywhere.

There was a saucepan full of hardened spaghetti perched on the small gas cooker. The front of the cooker itself was stained.

On the fridge there were a number of decorative magnets, one of which lit up when the door was opened. It was of a topless girl, and when it was moved the nipples glowed bright red for a second or two.

'You live like a fucking pig,' Stephen Kirkland

said, glancing round the room. 'Don't you ever clean this place?'

'I didn't ask you here so you could comment on my standards of fucking hygiene.' Constable Paul Rowley eyed Kirkland warily across the table.

'Just as well.' Kirkland sneered. 'Now tell me what's so important.'

'Your brother's grave,' Rowley began quietly. 'It was dug up. His body was taken.'

'What do you mean, taken?'

'There's something going on here in Darworth. Somebody called it voodoo. It's the blacks—'

'Voodoo?'

'Some kind of religion they practise. I can't remember the name of it.'

'Some fucking nigger dug up my brother and stole his body?'

'His grave and eight others were tampered with. Other bodies were taken as well.'

Kirkland gripped the beer bottle in his hand so hard it seemed it would break.

'Where's Gary's body?' he demanded.

'No one knows. That's what I said. It was taken.'

'Cunts,' roared Kirkland, leaping to his feet. He hurled the beer bottle at the sink, where it shattered. Fragments of glass and spilled beer exploded in all directions.

'And Bishop knows about this?' Kirkland seethed. 'He fucking knows and he's done fuck all?'

'They're questioning the Africans—' Rowley began, seeing the fury in Kirkland's eyes.

'Questioning them? Fucking questioning them? Jesus Christ!'

'I thought you had a right to know.'

Kirkland gripped the edge of the table, his breath coming in deep inhalations that caused his nostrils to flare like a raging bull's.

'I'm going to fucking kill them all,' he said quietly. 'Every last one of the black cunts.'

'You can't let anyone know I told you, Steve. It's just that I knew Gary and, well, like I said, I thought you had a right to know.'

'Who else knows?'

'The pathologist, DC Hall—'

'What about that black bastard Pearson?' Kirkland demanded. 'The news bloke. The nigger on the telly? He's been up Bishop's arse since he fucking got here. Does he know?'

'Yeah.'

Kirkland made for the back door, pulling it open angrily.

'Don't tell anyone I told you, Steve,' Rowley called after him.

Kirkland was already gone.

56

'She rang this morning,' Pearson said, glancing at his watch. 'About two hours ago.'

'And you're sure it was the same woman?' DS Bishop asked, reaching for the styrofoam cup of coffee on his desk.

'It was Emily Juma,' Pearson told him, sitting back in his seat and glancing around the detective's office. 'She wants me to meet her this afternoon at four.'

'Why didn't she contact us? Why not notify the police in the first place?'

'She says she trusts me. All I can think is that it's because we're the same colour.'

Bishop raised one eyebrow quizzically. 'You've got about as much in common with those Africans as I have with the Duke of fucking Edinburgh,' he said.

'Does it matter why, Bishop? She might have some information that will help your investigation

– help you find those missing kids. That's all that matters, isn't it?'

Bishop nodded. 'I've decided to put Mowende under surveillance,' he said. 'Effective as of now.'

'Good idea. Did he say anything useful when you interviewed him?'

'He's a slippery bastard. He doesn't scare easily. But then again, you'd know that, wouldn't you?'

Pearson held the policeman's gaze.

'Just what is it between you and Mowende?' Bishop wanted to know. 'How come you know so much about him?'

'I told you, I was a foreign correspondent. I covered Africa mainly. I crossed paths with Mowende a few times. I interviewed him when he was in charge of an army unit in Liberia. And again when he was running as a presidential candidate in Sierra Leone.'

'Did you know then about his links with Uthalande?'

'He never kept it a secret. He didn't feel he had to. There are nearly as many religions in Africa as there are people. Some probably worse than Uthalande. It was never an issue.'

'A religion that calls for human sacrifice and the killing of children was never an issue?'

Pearson shook his head.

'Then why was Mowende arrested and charged with murder in Sierra Leone?' the detective demanded.

'Because one of his victims was the daughter of the French High Commissioner. A white kid.'

Bishop eyed the newsman unblinkingly.

'Hundreds of thousands of Africans have been slaughtered in tribal and religious wars for decades,' Pearson said. 'No one takes much notice. Politicians in Europe and America make all the right noises about being outraged but no one really cares because Africa hasn't got the natural resources that the developed world needs.' He sighed. 'Do you think that the Americans would have invaded Iraq if its chief export had been bananas?'

'What the fuck are you talking about?'

'The Americans invaded Iraq because it's got huge reserves of oil. They said Saddam Hussein was a tyrant who had to be removed. Saddam was a saint compared to some of the African leaders. But did the Americans or the British intervene in the Congo or Nigeria or Liberia? No. Because those countries had nothing they wanted. It took the killing of a white child to get any action against Mowende.'

'That remark could be taken as racist.'

Pearson smiled. 'You're probably right,' he admitted. 'Maybe I'm just bitter – he tried to kill me too.'

'Why would he do that?'

'I wrote a series of articles and fronted some programmes on TV about him, implicating him in a series of massacres and assassinations. Tribal leaders who'd opposed him, and politicians too, had been murdered.'

'What happened?'

'I was working in a town called Shenge, in Sierra Leone, covering some local elections. Some of Mowende's cronies opened fire on the car we were in. My cameraman was killed. A sound guy and a journalist for CNN were cut up with machetes. I was wounded in the shoulder and back.'

'How long ago was that?'

'Six years.'

A silence descended on the room, finally broken by Bishop.

'Hell of a coincidence,' he mused. 'Six years ago Mowende tries to have you killed. Now he turns up here. Your luck stinks, doesn't it?'

Pearson smiled and got to his feet.

'Call me when you've spoken to Emily Juma,' Bishop said. 'Tell me what she said.'

Pearson nodded.

'And Pearson,' the policeman added. 'You watch yourself.'

57

'Did he actually say it was the Africans?'

Stephen Kirkland heard the question but he seemed intent on the task he was engaged in.

'Steve,' Raymond Carlton persisted. 'Did Rowley say that the black bastards were the ones who dug up the graves?'

'He did,' Kirkland said.

Carlton watched as the older man continued to pour petrol from the large metal can into the third of six smaller, five-litre plastic containers. The smell of the fuel was overpowering inside the confines of the garage, stronger even than the smell of oil and damp wood that permeated the air.

'What are we going to do?' Paul Duggan wanted to know, watching as Kirkland screwed the cap on to the container and lifted it into the boot of his car with the others.

'I don't know what you're going to do,' Kirkland

breathed, filling a fourth plastic receptacle. 'I'm going to burn those fucking flats to the ground, like I should have done eighteen months ago.'

'But what if we're wrong?' Carlton enquired. 'What if it's not them? Rowley might have been wrong.'

'Rowley hates niggers nearly as much as I do. Just because he's a copper doesn't mean he's changed. Why do you think he told me what happened at the cemetery the other night? He knows Bishop won't do anything about it.'

'Rowley's a cunt. He talks shit most of the time,' Carlton persisted.

'You losing your bottle, Ray?' Kirkland demanded, careful not to spill any of the petrol.

'No, I'm just saying—'

'Those black cunts dug my brother up,' Kirkland hissed, cutting across the younger man. 'First one of them murdered him and now they've fucked with his grave and with his memory. Now you can do what you fucking like but I'm telling you, tonight I'm going to turn those flats into fucking ash and with a bit of luck I'll kill all those black cunts that live there. If you want to help me then that's great. If not, you stay out of my fucking way otherwise I'll burn you too. Got that?'

58

'We cannot stay here,' Emily Juma protested, looking anxiously about her. 'Someone will see us. They will be watching.'

Nick Pearson saw the fear in the African woman's eyes and he reached out a comforting hand. Emily Juma pulled her arm away, her wide eyes scanning the area outside the windows of the café.

'There's no one watching, Emily,' Pearson said reassuringly.

'You don't know that.'

'You've got to tell me why you rang me. Is it about your daughter?'

Emily nodded almost imperceptibly.

'Why do you think she was taken?' Pearson asked quietly.

Emily kept her head low and didn't speak.

'Do you think it could be something to do with Uthalande?' Pearson murmured.

Emily Juma looked straight at him, eyes that already looked set to explode from their sockets now virtually incandescent.

'Is someone at the Western Road flats practising Uthalande?' Pearson continued. 'Are there followers of it living there?'

'How do you know about it?' Emily enquired, aghast.

'That's not important. What I do know is that human sacrifices are sometimes made by its followers. Do you think that's why Wanza has been taken?'

'I cannot speak of it.'

'If you want your daughter back alive you'll have to,' Pearson said. 'Am I right about a human sacrifice being made in some ceremonies?'

Emily nodded and closed her long fingers round her teacup.

'If the High Priest is trying to raise Him,' she said, her words barely audible.

'Raise who?' Pearson sat forward on his seat.

The African woman said something but Pearson didn't catch it.

'Who?'

'Isanwayo,' she repeated a little more loudly.

Pearson frowned.

'There are many gods who are worshipped in Uthalande but He is the most powerful of all. The most feared. To you, He would be Satan.'

'And who has the power to raise this . . . god?'

'Only the High Priest and then only with the offering of a sacrifice.'

'Can the High Priest raise the dead as well? Bring them back to life?'

Emily nodded.

'What happens at one of those ceremonies, Emily?'

The African woman shook her head repeatedly.

'You've got to tell me,' Pearson snapped. 'Do you want your daughter to die?'

'In my country, the followers gather on the orders of the High Priest,' Emily began slowly. 'A sacrifice has already been chosen. The High Priest speaks the words and offers the blood of the sacrifice to Isanwayo.'

'What happens to the sacrifice?'

'It depends what the High Priest has asked for. Sometimes he asks for the next harvest to be good. Or he asks for power over certain people. He can even ask for their deaths. Or he will ask Isanwayo himself to appear. If He does He can take human form.' Emily looked shame-facedly at Pearson then continued, her voice lower. 'The sacrifice is thrown from a high place, or the High Priest cuts out their heart. Sometimes he eats it.'

'Have you ever seen this ceremony carried out in this country, Emily?' he asked. 'Since you arrived here?'

The African woman shook her head.

'Why would anyone want to perform it now?' Pearson wanted to know.

'Revenge. A way of fighting back against the enemy.'

'Who's the enemy?'

'The white men who have persecuted us.'

'We've got to find your daughter.'

'I know where she is,' Emily murmured. 'Come to the flats tonight.'

'What time?' Pearson asked.

'Nine o'clock,' she told him, getting to her feet. 'There is a basement. I will meet you there. Away from those who watch.'

Pearson nodded. He was about to say something else when Emily Juma swept out of the café.

Pearson reached for his mobile phone and dialled.

59

The stench was unbearable.

Stephen Kirkland put one hand to his face to protect his nostrils from the noxious odour. It was a rank, fetid stink that reminded him of excrement and rotten meat.

He looked at the broken brickwork through which he'd entered the basement flats and wondered why the fresh air hadn't caused the worst of the odour to dissipate.

Not that any of that would matter soon, he told himself.

Outside the hole there was a short flight of concrete steps leading down to the front door of the long-abandoned flats. It was down those steps that Kirkland had come earlier. There had been no one around as he'd walked across the small open area at the side of the block. The security lights there weren't working anyway and Kirkland had moved through the gloom with speed and determination. Several swift blows with a sledgehammer had holed the rotten brickwork easily, allowing him a swifter entry than through the heavy metal door. He'd brought two of the petrol cans with him, and he was confident that his presence had gone unnoticed.

Kirkland smiled to himself. None of those who lived above would ever know he'd been below them until the flames really took hold and, by that time, it would be too late.

He was confident that two canisters of petrol would be enough.

Two in each block.

There was more than enough debris littered around in the basement flats for the flames to feed on once they began. The units in the long-abandoned kitchens were wood, as were the interior doors. They might be damp but they'd still burn.

Kirkland flicked on the torch he was carrying and shone the beam around.

He was standing in what had once been the living room of the subterranean flat. The walls were streaked black with mould. The concrete floor was visible through the threadbare carpet. Kirkland picked up one of the petrol cans and moved slowly across the room to the door. He pushed it open with his shoulder and saw that it led out into a small hallway. There was more carpet here. That, he reasoned, would also burn easily once he set light to the petrol.

What had served as a front door when the flats had been inhabited was still locked.

Kirkland kicked it hard and it collapsed outwards, the hinges simply tearing away from the rotten wood of the frame.

The crash reverberated around the subterranean level. Kirkland shone the torch to his left, aiming it down what was a long corridor. So long that the beam of the torch couldn't quite illuminate the end of it. Kirkland, still carrying the petrol can, made his way along the corridor.

The floor beneath him was bare concrete and slippery in places from the mould and damp that had seeped into it over the years.

He advanced further along the corridor, occasionally aiming the torch beam at the ground to ensure he didn't trip on the rubbish that was scattered liberally around. There were a number of rotting cardboard boxes outside one flat door. The broken tubes of fluorescent lights lay all around and he could hear the glass crunching beneath his feet as he walked.

As he passed the doors of the other flats he pushed against them, wondering if any were unlocked. He was beginning to wonder if it might be a better idea to pile as much flammable material as he could find in the middle of the corridor and light that. If he got one big blaze going then he'd be sure it would spread.

He considered the wisdom of this theory as he

continued to advance through the impenetrable blackness.

The torch beam glinted on something about twenty feet away.

It took Kirkland a moment to realise that it was one of the lift doors.

That was another possibility, he reasoned. Fill one of the lifts with rubbish and set fire to it. Once the blaze took hold it would shoot straight up the lift shaft to the floors above.

He grinned.

He had so many options.

The idea of building a bonfire in the corridor itself, however, seemed the most appealing to him. He decided to check a couple of the other underground flats for stuff to add to the coming conflagration.

Kirkland put his shoulder against the nearest door and pushed. It was locked.

He put down the petrol can, took a step back and drove his foot hard against the door. It creaked and split from top to bottom under the impact. He kicked at it again and the whole thing came away from the frame.

Kirkland picked it up and tossed it into the middle of the corridor, then he moved inside the flat.

He heard a high-pitched squeaking and saw a small rat scurry away, anxious to be out of the glaring white light of the torch beam. He watched it disappear through a hole in the skirting board.

Kirkland moved into the hallway of the flat and

then on into the kitchen. He propped the torch on the battered worktop and got a firm grip on the wooden cupboard above it.

He pulled and it came free easily, several large lumps of plaster coming away with it. Kirkland carried it back out into the corridor and dumped it on top of the broken door he'd already laid there.

He pulled three more of the units from the kitchen wall and piled them in the corridor as well. Then he did the same with the drawers, forming a pleasingly large pile.

When he was satisfied it was big enough he doused the whole lot with petrol, grateful that the pungent odour of the fuel seemed to be overpowering even the vile stench that filled the subterranean area.

Kirkland wiped his face. He was sweating. He decided to go back into the flat to see if there was anything in the abandoned living room that he could add to his pyre.

He pushed the door open and swept the room with the torch beam.

There was an old two-seater sofa in one corner of the room. That should make a fine addition to the bonfire, he thought. He was about to step into the room when he noticed the hole in the wall.

It was large. Twice as big as a man.

He took a step into the living room and shone the torch at the hole. He didn't think the masonry there had crumbled with neglect. It looked as if the hole had been made deliberately.

Kirkland crossed to it, aimed the torch into it and peered through.

The hole led into the living room of the next flat.

He stepped through.

This was too much to hope for, he told himself, grinning. If there were holes like this in the other walls then the fire he was soon to light would spread all the more quickly.

Kirkland chuckled.

He made his way to the front door of the flat and turned the handle. This one was unlocked and he found himself back in the corridor once again.

Somewhere in the blackness he heard a high-pitched squeal.

For a moment he wondered if it was another rat but the sound was too prolonged. Too strident. It seemed to be coming from the far end of the under-ground corridor, close to the flat where he'd first entered.

Had someone seen him and followed him down here?

He walked slowly back in the direction of the sound.

If it was one of the black bastards who lived above, he'd end up on the fucking bonfire with the other rubbish.

Kirkland smiled at the thought.

Suddenly he realised the sound was the creaking hinges of another door. He shone the torch around.

Nothing.

Perhaps it had been a rat, but—

The door to the flat opposite was open.

Kirkland pushed it with his foot and it swung gently back. He waited a moment, then stepped across the threshold.

The smell inside was so strong, so vile, that it made Kirkland retch. He felt his stomach contract and, for a second, he thought he was going to vomit.

He shone the torch at the kitchen door and saw that it too was open.

The smell must be coming from in there, he reasoned. There must be some rotten food or a dead animal somewhere. That was the only way to explain such an appalling stench.

Out in the corridor there was another sound, louder this time.

The sound of a door being slammed shut.

Kirkland stepped back out into the corridor and extended his arm, jabbing the torch into the blackness.

He hurried down the corridor towards the hastily built pile of rotten wood he'd assembled. He picked up the petrol can that lay close by and, holding it in one hand, walked backwards leaving a trail of fuel on the sticky concrete.

Satisfied that the can was empty he tossed it aside and dug his hand into his pocket. He pulled out a box of matches and struck one.

'Fucking burn, you bastards,' he hissed, gazing at the glowing match.

He dropped it and the petrol immediately caught light.

Flame chased along the trail of fuel until it reached the rotten wood piled high in the corridor.

There was a dull whump as the fuel-soaked heap ignited, filling the corridor with sickly yellow and orange light.

Kirkland grinned and backed off into the doorway of the flat he'd first entered. For long moments he watched the blaze as it took hold. Flames spread quickly to the walls and ceiling, devouring the flaking paint. The corridor was now also filling with billowing smoke.

Kirkland squinted beyond the growing blaze, his attention caught by more movement down by the lift doors.

But this was no rat. This was something much bigger. The size of a man.

One of the bastards must have seen him come down here and followed him and now he was going to be the first to burn.

'Die, you black cunt,' Kirkland shouted venomously, his face twisted into a grimace.

It was time to repeat his task in the second and third buildings. As he turned to leave he caught that rank stench again and, as before, he almost vomited it was so intense.

The figure that loomed into view came from his

left, from the kitchen. Kirkland aimed the torch at its face.

'Oh, Jesus,' he choked, his eyes bulging madly in their sockets.

The figure took a step towards him.

60

'She said nine o'clock,' Pearson said as he swung himself out of the car. He checked his watch. 'It's just after.'

Bishop shut his own door and locked the Astra, gazing up at the high-rise columns of the three massive concrete pillars making up the Western Road flats.

'No lights,' the detective noted, his eyes scanning the many windows and walkways that towered above. 'No lights anywhere.'

'Power cut?' Pearson suggested.

'No one around either,' Bishop said as they walked towards the main entrance of the central block. 'I can't imagine everyone's in bed at this time.'

'Perhaps they've all moved out,' Pearson offered.

Bishop looked dismissively at the journalist and pushed open the door.

The footsteps of the two men echoed on the

tiled floor of the entryway. Pearson gazed around. He saw the graffiti on the wall close to the lifts:

BLACK CUNTS

'Kirkland?' he asked, nodding in the direction of the spray-painted letters.

'Or one of his little gang.' Bishop sighed. 'Mind you, they're not the only ones who might have done it. Kirkland's not alone in thinking the way he does about these people.'

Pearson wandered over to the lift doors. He pulled at the rusty padlock and chains that were fastened across the entrance.

'Who put these here?' he wanted to know.

'The council,' Bishop told him. 'When the basement flats were condemned they didn't want people going down there. No one's lived down there for ten years.'

'Is there another way down apart from the lifts?'

'Stairs,' Bishop said, pointing to a set of double doors away to the left.

'How come that entrance isn't padlocked?'

'How the hell should I know?' Bishop snapped. 'I told you, it was a council decision.'

Pearson walked towards the double doors and pulled at the handles.

'They're open,' he muttered. 'The bolts are undone.' The partitions moved, allowing him a view of a concrete staircase leading downwards. The dust on the other side of the doors was thick, as it was on the steps themselves and on the handrails. 'And you've never searched the basement flats when you've been here?'

'I told you,' Bishop repeated wearily, wandering across to join the journalist. 'No one's lived in the fucking things for more than ten years.'

Pearson pointed at something close to the double doors.

'Maybe not,' he said. 'But someone's been down there recently. Those are footprints, aren't they?'

Bishop crouched down to examine the indentations in the dust.

'There are more on the stairs,' he murmured.

'Do you want me to have a look in the basement while you check the other floors?' Pearson offered.

Bishop hesitated a moment.

'There's no electricity down there. You won't be able to see a hand in front of you,' he said. 'I've got a couple of torches in the car. I'll go and get them.'

He wheeled round and hurried out of the main doors.

Pearson took a step closer to the top of the stairs that led down to the basement flats, scanning the marks in the thick dust.

The footprints were smaller than his own.

A woman's?

But the others that had disturbed the thick coating of dust and grime were tinier still. They could only have been made by a child, he reasoned.

A missing child?

Pearson squinted into the impenetrable gloom at the bottom of the stairs. It was impossible to see what lay below. He coughed and waved a hand in front of his face as some of the dust he'd disturbed rose in a noxious cloud. He decided to step back into the well-lit entryway until Bishop returned with the torches.

It was as he took a step back that he heard a sound from below him.

Pearson froze for a second, his ears straining to detect the noise again. He crossed quickly back to the top of the stairs, leaning forward over the handrail.

The sound came once more.

High-pitched. Shrill.

A voice?

'Here, take this.'

He spun round as Bishop returned and shoved a torch into his hand. He switched it on immediately and shone it over the handrail down into the thick blackness below.

'Why the hell did Emily Juma want to meet me down there?' he murmured, still staring into the gloom.

'Let's go and find out,' Bishop muttered.

61

Stephen Kirkland shook his head in horrified disbelief as he stumbled backwards.

His entire body was shuddering uncontrollably
and the torch he held shook so violently it looked
as if the face of the figure before him was lit with
a strobe.

But, in that madly dancing light, he could see
only too clearly the features of the figure.

They were unmistakably those of his dead brother.

'Gary,' Kirkland breathed.

The figure didn't answer. It merely continued to
move towards him. And, as it did so, Kirkland was
assaulted by that foul stench. It clogged in his nostrils,
making every breath difficult. Breath that he was
finding hard enough to take anyway. The sight before
him seemed to have paralysed his lungs. He couldn't
suck in enough oxygen.

He recognised the suit his brother had been buried

in, though the navy blue material had faded some-what and it was covered in dried mud and other dark stains, some of which looked like congealed blood.

He could see that the skin on his brother's face was grey in colour. It looked too thin, stretched almost to breaking point over the bones. Gary's lips were purple, as was the flesh beneath his eyes. It was the eyes that drew Kirkland's attention most of all. They were gleaming in the torch beam but that was because they were almost liquescent. The corneas were virtually opaque apart from the tiny pupils that looked like black dots in the midst of the whiteness.

There was more mud on the face and forearms, some beneath nails that were either broken or missing. And, all over both hands, there was dried blood.

Kirkland continued to back away, not wanting to believe what he saw. Not able to comprehend what was happening.

But somewhere amidst the fear that gripped him there was a terrible sadness.

He could see his brother but he was sure that his sibling couldn't see him. Or, if he could, he had no idea whom he was looking at. Whether those putres-cent, cataract-covered orbs were capable of sight, Kirkland had no idea. All he knew was that he was staring at the visage of a loved one he had last seen alive eighteen months earlier.

That revelation alone was enough to send him spinning off into madness. The fact that the figure was drawing closer to him only compounded the insanity.

'Gary, it's me,' Kirkland gasped.

The figure lunged at him and closed both hands round his throat, slamming him back against the flimsy wall.

At first, Kirkland didn't fight back. His mind was able to process only the fact that the hands that gripped him belonged to the brother he had loved so much.

However, as the fingers squeezed more tightly, he struck out with the torch. It caught his brother on the temple but the blow did nothing to alleviate the pressure on Kirkland's throat. If anything, the reeking fingers only pressed harder.

Kirkland struck out again but his brother roared defiantly, his mouth gaping open to expel noxious air from rotting lungs.

Kirkland felt himself being lifted off his feet. He kicked out hard and caught his brother in the stomach.

The thing that had been Gary dropped Kirkland and stumbled backwards slightly but it was only seconds before it rushed at him again. The impact sent both of them crashing into the corridor beyond. They fell to the floor, Kirkland's brother landing on top of him, hands fastening round his neck again.

Kirkland could feel the heat from the fire that

was spreading rapidly along the corridor, but it seemed unimportant compared to the pressure on his throat. White stars danced before his eyes and he felt unconsciousness beginning to wash over him.

He tried to shout something, tried to say his brother's name, but the figure raised Kirkland's head a few inches from the floor then slammed it down again with terrifying force. Kirkland heard a crack and realised that it was his own skull.

He felt sick, but the bile that rushed up his throat was held there by the vice-like grip on his windpipe. He struck at the eyes of his attacker, but even though the two fingers he drove forward tore through one watery orb and punctured the skull as deep as the second knuckle, they had no effect. There was no relief from the pressure on Kirkland's throat and, at last, his efforts became weaker. He could taste blood and realised that he'd bitten through his own tongue.

Above him, his brother opened his mouth once again and roared something, but Kirkland barely heard it. All he was aware of now was the heat that was drawing nearer. Flames were licking along the walls close to him. The smoke filled his lungs.

One last portion of his mind capable of thought hoped he would be dead before the fire reached him. That agony would surely be too much.

62

Motes of dust turned lazily in the beams of the two torches. Pearson aimed the one he held at the floor while Bishop directed the light slowly back and forth.

'Are you sure she wanted to meet you down here?' the detective said as they reached the bottom of the concrete steps.

'Yes,' Pearson told him, catching the note of disdain in the other man's voice.

'These footprints could have been made days ago,' Bishop went on. 'And why didn't she say *which* basement?'

'I heard movement down here,' Pearson snapped. 'If you think I'm hearing things then leave me to search on my own.'

Bishop shone his torch into Pearson's face. 'You check that side,' the detective said, gesturing to his right. 'I'll do these.' He inclined his head towards the row of doors on the left. 'If you find anything, shout.'

'How do we get in?'

Bishop didn't speak, but merely turned to the door nearest him and pressed it with his hand. When it wouldn't open he drove one foot against the wood. The door slammed back against the wall behind, yawning open to expose the flat's hallway.

Pearson nodded and turned towards his own objective.

'When you've checked each one, wait for me,' Bishop instructed. 'Otherwise we'll lose each other down here. Got it?'

Pearson put his weight against the door he faced and found it was open. He pushed it and stepped forward into the deserted basement flat. Opposite him, Bishop also advanced. Almost palpable darkness flooded back into the corridor as the two torches disappeared.

As he stepped into the narrow hallway, Pearson shone his torch around, allowing the powerful beam to pick out doors to his left, his right and straight ahead. He took the one to his left first.

It opened into a small kitchen.

There was still a metal, formica-topped table standing in one corner of the room and, he noted, a rusted cat bowl. Apart from those the room was empty. He backed out and checked the door behind him.

It was a bathroom.

Pearson shone his torch at the old enamelled bath and winced when he saw that the bottom of it was covered by a layer of dirt and dust fully two inches thick. There was a dark brown stain from the base of the taps down to the plughole. The toilet was in a similar state, the water having dried up long ago. He saw a cockroach crawl effortlessly down the pan and out of sight.

There were thick cobwebs on the cistern and in every corner of the room. These too were covered in dust and Pearson could only guess how long they'd been there.

He backed out of the bathroom and checked the rooms ahead of him.

To his right lay a bedroom, the frame of the bed still intact. There were some battered wooden drawers pushed up against a wall but, apart from those last reminders that this place had once been inhabited, the bedroom was empty.

The space to his left had been the living room, and as he shone his torch over the far wall he noticed that there was a hole in the plaster about three feet across.

Pearson crossed to it and shone his torch into it, surprised to see that it led into the bedroom of the next flat.

He wondered, for brief seconds, about pulling himself through into the adjoining chamber but decided against it and headed out into the main corridor again instead.

Bishop was already waiting for him.

'Nothing,' the detective said wearily. 'All I found was dirt, dust and rat shit.'

'Same here,' Pearson admitted. 'There was a hole in the living-room wall, though. It led through into the bedroom of that flat.' He pointed to the next door on the left. 'I wonder why?'

Bishop merely shook his head.

Pearson shone his torch up the corridor but the blackness was so total that the beam couldn't penetrate very far.

'Let's check the next two,' Bishop said.

They moved on.

Despite the lack of oxygen and the thick dust in the air of the subterranean flats, the flames had found ample nourishment from the petrol Stephen Kirkland had used. Having devoured the wooden cupboards and doors he'd piled up, the conflagration had spread rapidly to the walls and ceiling, igniting the paint there. Choking smoke filled the corridor as the flames destroyed everything they touched. The bodies of Kirkland himself and his brother were simply more fuel for the roaring blaze, consumed easily by the inferno.

In the basement flats of the first tower block, the fire grew more intense as it engulfed everything in its path.

63

Every flat, Pearson reasoned as he pushed open the door of the next kitchen, must be the same shape. Every room must share the same dimensions. Four moderately sized chambers, built like boxes and stacked like huge concrete and glass building bricks.

Unlike the first flat he'd investigated, he found that the next contained ample evidence of its previous inhabitants. There was some dried-out makeup in the bathroom, even an old safety razor on the cracked glass shelf above the sink. Dried-up bottles of shampoo and bubble bath had also been left on the side of the bath. In the kitchen, there were old plates piled on the rusted draining board and some knives and forks in the sink.

As he wandered into the bedroom, Pearson was again drawn to the hole in the wall that connected this flat with the first he'd been into.

He inspected the edges of the hole, running his

thumb over the chipped plaster there. Some small pieces came away, adding more particles of dust to air that was already clogged with the stuff. The journalist coughed and backed away.

Against the far wall of the room there was a camp bed, complete with a mouldy-looking mattress. A child's toy rabbit, threadbare and missing both eyes, lay discarded on it. Stuffing had been pulled from the toy, the foam rubber protruding from its belly like spongy entrails.

Pearson retreated from the bedroom into the living room.

As he did so, his torch dimmed slightly. The beam dipped from its usual brilliant whiteness to a dull orange.

'Shit,' he murmured, and shook it angrily. The light returned with its customary brilliance and Pearson moved on.

'What the hell . . .' he whispered as he shone the torch round the living room.

There was another hole in the wall opposite him, this one easily big enough for him to get through.

'Decaying plaster, eh?' he muttered to himself, shaking his head.

If he was right and all the flats were laid out the same way, then this hole should lead directly into the bedroom of the next flat. He crossed to it and shone the torch through to test his theory. The beam illuminated the bedroom just as he'd suspected it would.

Pearson crouched down and stepped through the hole with ease, standing upright again when he was in the adjacent flat.

Who had done this and why?

He moved quickly through the next bedroom, into the living room and then to the kitchen. None of them showed anything other than filth and neglect. He pushed open the bathroom door.

Something brushed his face.

Pearson jerked backwards, swatting at the object with his free hand. With a combination of anger and disgust he realised that it was a dead spider.

'Shit,' he panted, pointing the torch at the long-legged creature now lying at his feet.

He managed a smile at his own nervousness. He sucked in several lungfuls of the stale and musty air, his heart still thumping against his ribs, and steadied himself before heading for the front door of the flat.

Bishop would probably be waiting outside in the corridor for him again.

Pearson found that the flat door was locked from the inside.

Just as well you came through the wall, eh?

He smiled to himself and unlocked the door, stepping out into the corridor.

As he did so, the figure lunged at him.

64

Pearson shot up his hand to ward off the attack, swinging wildly with the torch in the process. It smacked hard against the temple of his assailant, and the corridor was plunged into total darkness.

In that impenetrable gloom, Pearson was aware of an overpowering stench and also of low guttural breathing. Blind in the blackness, he had little chance to prepare himself for the next attack.

It came from his right.

He felt hands grabbing at his face and neck and, in the gloom, thought that he was being attacked by more than one person. However, as he struck out wildly with his fists, he realised that there was just one assailant. One that he couldn't see.

The smell was overwhelming. It filled Pearson's nostrils as his attacker slammed him back against the wall, trying to fix bony fingers round his throat.

The journalist knocked one of the hands away.

'Bishop,' he roared at the top of his voice. 'Help me.'

He was struck in the side of the face by something he couldn't make out. Something that split his eyebrow. Pearson felt blood run down his face and he crashed to the ground.

He kicked out blindly, guessing that his attacker was close by.

How can he see me if I can't see him?

'Bishop,' he shouted again.

The door of the flat opposite burst open and the beam of Bishop's torch cut through the darkness. The light illuminated Pearson's attacker.

'Jesus,' hissed Bishop as he saw what was happening.

Pearson tried to roll away from his assailant, crawling over the dusty, dirt-encrusted floor. The detective kept his torch aimed at the other figure and it stood motionless for a second then turned to face him.

Bishop thought, for one fleeting second, that there was something horribly familiar about the man who faced him. But he knew that what was illuminated in the beam of his torch was no man. Perhaps it had been once, but no more. The vision before him was plucked straight from a nightmare.

The blackened flesh was peeling away from the bones of the face. The teeth gleamed whitely against the charred mass of skin and the incinerated lips. The ribs were exposed in places, and all over the body there were smudges of dried earth and blood.

Pearson scrambled towards the door through which he'd just emerged, feeling his way in the blackness. His aim was to get away from this monstrosity but also to reach the knives he'd seen in the neighbouring flat. Anything that could be used as a weapon. Exactly how he was going to reach them in the darkness he had no idea. All he knew was he must get to them.

As he moved, the figure leapt at him again. Bishop struck at it with his own torch and what little light had illuminated the monstrous scene disappeared completely. Neither of the men could see a hand in front of them.

Pearson felt a crushing weight on his legs as Bishop and the other creature fell to the ground, but he didn't dare kick out in case he struck the policeman.

Find the torch.

He had to have enough light to see where to strike.

In the enveloping gloom he reached out helplessly in an attempt to find one of the dropped torches. It was hopeless.

A cacophony of sounds reached his ears: the furious grunting of Bishop as he tried to fight the creature off, the figure's own laboured breathing and mucoid raspings and the sound of his own frantic gasps.

'Get it off me,' Bishop snarled somewhere in the gloom. The words were cut short by a rattling wheeze and Pearson thought that the creature had seized Bishop by the throat.

Do something. Think.

Pearson dug his hand hastily into his jacket pocket and pulled out his lighter. He flicked it on and in the flickering flame he saw the nightmare tableau.

The creature had locked its hands round Bishop's throat and was attempting to throttle him.

Pearson raised the lighter high into the air, the puddle of sickly yellow light spreading wider, and kicked hard at the creature. He connected with its face.

There was a sharp crack that he recognised as breaking bone and the creature fell sideways, several of its teeth spilling from its mouth. It gave Bishop enough time to roll sideways, away from its next attack.

Pearson saw one of the dropped torches and grabbed for it, flicking it on again and shining it into the creature's face. Momentarily blinded by the light, it recoiled, and Bishop struck at it, catching it on the jaw with a powerful punch. It stumbled backwards and the detective advanced upon it, lashing out again.

'Get something to kill it,' he gasped.

Pearson drove a foot into the nearest door. It cracked and he did it again, kicking madly until the wood splintered in three places. He tore a piece of it free and hefted it. The wooden stave was two feet long and it felt satisfyingly heavy to Pearson as he advanced on the figure.

'Take this,' he snapped, pushing the torch towards the detective, who did as he was asked, bringing the beam to bear on the monstrous vision before him.

Pearson struck at it twice with a power born of fear.

The first blow broke its right wrist. The second slammed into its face, shattering the cheekbone.

It dropped to its knees.

'Kill it,' Bishop bellowed.

Pearson swallowed hard, then brought the piece of wood down on the creature's skull with irresistible force.

The cranium split open like a ripe tomato, a portion of bone spinning away to reveal the brain beneath.

Pearson hit it again. And again.

In the flickering beam of the torch he rained blows on it until he barely had the strength to raise the lump of splintered wood. Only when he was sure there was no more movement from the body did he stop, dropping the wood to the ground beside it. Exhausted by his furious attack, he leaned back against the wall, gasping for breath.

Bishop, massaging his bruised and scratched throat with one hand, aimed the torch at the shattered face of the motionless figure.

'The first body that disappeared from the morgue,' he panted, his eyes fixed on the corpse at his feet. 'Emmanuel Agassa. That's him.' He prodded the dead African with the toe of his shoe.

'A servant,' Pearson whispered.

'There'll be others,' the detective said. 'I thought you said a body reanimated by Uthalande didn't decay.'

'Supposedly decay is stopped or can be reversed,' Pearson replied. 'Obviously not in every case.'

Bishop shook the torch as the light from it dimmed a little. He flashed it round the corridor, the beam picking out the other one. Pearson reached for it and flicked the switch.

Nothing happened.

'The impact must have damaged it,' he breathed desperately.

'If there are more of those things down here we'd better stay together anyway,' Bishop said. 'Keep the torch. It'll do as a weapon.'

They prepared to move on.

'Wait,' Pearson suddenly hissed. 'Put the torch out.'

Bishop looked at him in bewilderment.

'Put it out,' Pearson insisted.

The detective did as he was asked.

'Look, there,' Pearson whispered, pointing ahead. 'One of the flats near the end of the corridor. There's light coming under the door.'

The corridor in the basement of the first block of flats was an inferno. From one end to the other it blazed, the flames incinerating everything they touched.

Doors were turned to charcoal as the fire spewed

into the flats themselves, moving like a predator seeking out more material to devour.

Smoke began to fill the lift shaft and rise towards the floors above. The metal doors to the shaft began to buckle under the incredible temperatures generated within the corridor.

Less than one hour after the fire had begun, every empty dwelling in the basement of the first block of the Western Road flats was ablaze.

65

'Come on,' Pearson whispered. His gaze, like Bishop's, was riveted to the thin strip of light showing about thirty feet ahead of them. 'We've got to see what it is.'

'Probably more of those fucking things,' the detective hissed, aiming the torch swiftly at the motionless body of Emmanuel Agassa.

'We've got to see,' Pearson repeated, gripping his torch more firmly.

Bishop nodded and switched off their only source of light. The two men moved forward.

'I'm going to call for help,' Bishop murmured, reaching for his mobile. 'If there *are* more of those things down here then we need back-up.'

He flipped open the phone. NO SIGNAL flashed up on the screen.

'Shit,' hissed the detective. 'I suppose I should have known.' He slipped the mobile back into his jacket and continued to advance alongside Pearson.

The door was now only fifteen feet away. Beneath it, they could still clearly see the ribbon of light. It drew them as surely as a flame would draw a moth.

Or a spider a fly?

Pearson stepped close to the door and listened.

'Can't hear anything,' he whispered.

Bishop moved closer to him, his hand reaching out to rest against the door.

Both men were trying to control their breathing. Pearson put his hand to his head and wiped away some blood, feeling it on his fingertips.

'Try it,' he said as quietly as he could.

Bishop steadied himself and put his weight against the door. It swung open.

Both men stepped back, one on either side of the entrance. Yellow light flooded out into the corridor. It was enough to allow them to see each other's faces.

Bishop jabbed a finger towards the doorway of the flat and nodded. Pearson understood.

'Now,' the detective whispered.

Both men ducked into the hallway of the flat.

There were five candles on the floor of the small entryway, all lit and arranged in a rough X-shape.

'Why didn't we see the light when we first came down here?' Pearson murmured, staring at the candles.

'Because these weren't lit then,' Bishop said quietly. 'Otherwise we *would* have seen. And look' — he pointed at the candles — 'very little wax has burned. These were lit during the last couple of minutes.'

'Who by?' Pearson muttered to himself.

Bishop advanced towards the bathroom door and pushed it open.

Empty.

Pearson did the same with the kitchen.

Also empty.

Bishop moved towards the bedroom while Pearson approached the living room. They pushed the doors simultaneously.

'Here,' Bishop snapped, turning on the torch, and Pearson spun round, stepping alongside him, gazing at what the beam illuminated.

The African woman who stood before them was dressed in a long grey robe which had a cross drawn roughly on the front of it. The child standing in front of her wore a similar garment.

'He said you would come,' she said, smiling. 'This is my daughter, Wanza.' She stroked the little girl's hair and the child smiled too.

'Emily, what's going on?' Pearson said slowly. 'What about the other kids? There were two others missing as well.'

'They are with Him.'

'Where?'

'I told you. With Him,' Emily said, bowing her head slightly.

'A religion that involves human sacrifice,' Pearson murmured.

'What?' Bishop snapped.

'The child was to be a sacrifice,' Pearson said.

'That was what we were meant to think. That this child' – he pointed at the little girl – 'would be used in a Uthalande ceremony.'

Emily looked evenly at him, the smile still hovering on her lips.

'Your daughter was never going to be used as a sacrifice, was she, Emily?' Pearson said flatly.

Emily Juma shook her head.

'She was never a victim,' Pearson continued. 'She was bait. To bring us here.'

'What the fuck are you going on about?' snapped the DS. 'Bring us here for what?'

Pearson's eyes never left Emily Juma and her daughter.

'*We're* the sacrifices,' he breathed.

66

'The children will be first,' Emily Juma rasped.

As she spoke, she opened her long robe, spreading it wide like the wings of a huge bat. Pearson and Bishop saw that she was naked beneath it, her slender body illuminated by the faltering beam of the torch. However, there was enough light for them to see the three X-shaped scars on her breasts. Carved carefully just above the nipples, the cuts on the left breast still looked raw. Fresh.

'Oh, Christ,' Bishop murmured, looking on in horror as Emily's daughter imitated the movement, parting her own robe to reveal her childish nakedness. The cuts on her small body were just above the pubis. Three carefully gouged Xs, carved expertly into the flesh.

'We came here to live in peace,' Emily said, her face contorted with rage. 'But the whites would not let us. Because of them we have been forced to fight back the only way we know. Using our religion. Our gods.'

'Uthalande,' Pearson said.

'Yes,' she hissed, taking a step towards the two men.

'Where's Mowende? He's the High Priest, isn't he?'

'He is with the children.'

'Where are they?' Bishop demanded.

'You will not reach them in time,' the African woman snarled. 'By the time they fall it will be too late.'

'Fall?' Bishop snapped.

'From the heavens,' the African woman said, looking upwards. 'You will all die here.'

It was the child who ran at them.

Screaming like a banshee, the little girl threw herself at Bishop. The DS tried to avoid her but she butted him hard in the stomach. She fell on him, scratching at his face and trying to bite him. The torch spun from his hand and landed with a crash on the concrete floor, but the sickly yellow light given off by the candles lit the living room enough for Pearson to see the detective hurl the child away.

Immediately she rushed back at him, screaming madly. Emily followed, her hands outstretched, her long fingers reaching for Pearson's neck.

Pearson managed to catch her wrists and he used her own momentum to swing her round. He hurled her towards the open door as Bishop managed to grab the screaming child and lift her into the air, holding her away from him, struggling to keep a grip on her.

Emily sprang back at Pearson but he caught her with a perfect right hook. The blow split her top lip and knocked out a tooth. She staggered for a second then collapsed in the hallway, knocking over two of the candles. One of them fell against her robe and the flimsy material ignited immediately.

Bishop was still holding the child at arm's length, trying to avoid her powerful kicks and flailing arms. She scratched savagely at his hands and, with all his strength, he threw her towards the nearest wall.

She slammed against it like a rag doll, her head smacking sickeningly against the plaster. She dropped limply to the floor and lay still.

Flames had now destroyed the bottom part of Emily Juma's robe. They leapt high, feeding on both the material and her flesh. Pearson caught the acrid stench of burning skin but he could also smell something else. The rank, choking odour he had detected earlier, when Emmanuel Agassa had attacked him.

The fire that was engulfing Emily Juma illuminated several dark shapes in the corridor beyond the flat.

'The other servants,' he breathed. 'Mowende must keep them down here like fucking pets.'

He looked round and saw that the long-abandoned living room still contained a couple of broken wooden chairs. He hurried across to one and stamped hard on it, pulling a leg off. He handed it to Bishop and tore away part of the curved back for himself. It was only a foot long but it was thick and there was a screw sticking out of the end.

'Why don't those fucking things attack us?' the DS gasped.

'Perhaps they're frightened of the fire,' Pearson said. 'Either that or they know the only way we can get out is through them.'

The journalist gripped the piece of chair like a club and looked at Bishop, who was also brandishing his lump of splintered wood.

'Ready?' the detective breathed.

Pearson nodded. 'The fire might blind them long enough.'

The two men dashed frenziedly into the hallway.

67

The hallway was ablaze.

Walls and ceiling were covered in flames, as was the body of Emily Juma. Pearson and Bishop used their arms to shield their eyes as they passed through the rapidly growing conflagration. Pearson felt his hair ignite in places, his eyebrows singed by the fire and his skin momentarily scorched. But he and Bishop ploughed on, out of the inferno and into the corridor beyond.

Immediately they were aware of figures around them. Figures that snatched and grabbed at them, trying to wrestle them down. Both men struck out furiously to their right and left. Pearson felt the lump of wood he was holding connect with something solid in the flame-lit darkness. One of the figures fell backwards. Bishop kicked too, driving his foot into the shin of one of his attackers, slamming the chair leg down on to its neck.

Driven by fear and anger, the two men struck madly at their assailants. Pearson felt something wet splatter his face but he wasn't sure whether it was blood or sputum – his own or one of the creatures'.

'This way,' roared Bishop, pulling at the journalist's jacket, guiding him towards the flight of steps that would lead them out of the basement.

Pearson slipped and almost fell on the concrete floor but he bounced off a wall, regained his footing and ran on.

Three of the creatures ran after them.

The journalist looked back and saw them silhouetted against the deep red of the fire that was now beginning to burst out of the flat where it had begun. Tongues of flame licked hungrily at the roof of the corridor and smoke belched out in thick, noxious clouds.

Bishop made the staircase first, stumbling upwards towards the light. Pearson followed, swinging round to kick out at one of his pursuers. His foot connected with its stomach and the impact sent the creature tumbling backwards. It crashed into its two companions and all three fell heavily.

Ahead of him, Bishop had reached the double doors that they'd passed through to reach the basement flats. He crashed through them, skidding on the slippery floor. Pearson was seconds behind him.

Bishop was already punching out a number on his mobile phone.

Pearson stood watching the double doors, gasping

for breath, the bloodied piece of wood clutched in one hand. He had several splinters deep in the flesh of his palm but the pain seemed unimportant.

'I want as many men as possible to the Western Road flats now,' Bishop barked into the phone. 'And an ambulance and fire engines. As quick as you can. Do it.' He shouted the last two words then snapped the phone shut.

'The other two kids,' Pearson gasped, barely able to catch his breath.

'We don't know where they are.'

'Emily Juma said something about them being dead before they fell. Fell from the heavens.'

Bishop merely shook his head.

'The roof,' Pearson said. 'It has to be that. Mowende's got them on the roof.'

There was a thunderous crash from behind them and both men spun round.

The first of a series of heavy impacts landed on the doors to the basement.

'It won't take them long to get through,' Bishop said, wiping sweat from his face.

'Leave them,' Pearson said, bolting for the lift. 'Let's get to the roof.'

68

The lift rose with agonising slowness.

'Come on,' Pearson muttered. 'Come on.'

'It'd be quicker on foot,' Bishop snapped.

Another floor was reached.

And another.

'They'll be dead before we get to them,' the DS rasped. 'If they're even up here.'

'We've got to try,' Pearson said angrily.

The lift reached the top floor.

The two men hurried out, looking round for the short flight of service steps that would lead them up to the roof itself.

'There,' Bishop shouted, pointing to a pair of fire doors to their right. Both men bolted towards them, crashing through and hurtling up the stone steps beyond.

Bishop was the first to reach the wooden door separating them from the roof. He pushed against it and twisted the handle, realising angrily that it was locked. The detective kicked furiously at the handle, which flew off and rattled across the floor. The door swung open. A gust of cold air met them as they rushed out on to the roof, looking round anxiously in the darkness.

'Don't come any closer.'

Victor Mowende's voice boomed out in the gloom.

Pearson turned in the direction of the sound and saw the tall African standing close to the parapet, framed on either side by two tall metal ventilation ducts that reached as high as his waist. He seemed untroubled by the wind that was whistling around him, threatening to buffet him off his precipitous perch.

'Where are the children?' Bishop shouted, advancing a couple of steps.

'Stay back,' Pearson urged, grabbing the detective's arm. 'He'll kill them.'

Bishop continued advancing towards Mowende. 'I want to see them,' he called. 'I want to know they're still alive.'

'And what will you do if they are already dead?' the African asked.

'Dead like Emily Juma?' Pearson taunted him, walking up until he was level with Bishop. 'Dead like those things in the basement?'

Mowende eyed him warily for a moment then smiled again.

'Where they came from there are many more,' he said defiantly.

'Fuck you,' Bishop rasped. 'I'm going to kill you, you black bastard.'

'So, at last you show your true feelings,' Mowende chided him. 'Your true *colours.*' He laughed that mocking laugh once again. 'Is it any wonder the rest of the people in this town are so filled with hate?'

'Show me the kids,' Bishop repeated.

Mowende kept his eyes on the two men but reached down with his left hand. Pearson and Bishop watched as he hauled a small figure into view.

A black girl, her hands firmly bound with rope, stood before them, supported by Mowende's grip.

'More of my men will be here soon,' Bishop called. 'Your own people are in danger too from the fire in the basement of these flats. Let her go.'

'And what? You will forget everything?' Mowende grinned.

'You can't get away,' Pearson told him, moving forward a couple of paces.

'Perhaps I don't want to,' Mowende said.

He pulled his right hand into view and the two men saw that in it he was holding a straight-edged knife about ten inches long. He pressed the cutting edge to the girl's throat and held it there.

'Put the knife down and let her go,' Bishop shouted.

'No,' Mowende said flatly.

'What do you think you can achieve by killing her?' Pearson asked. 'Do you want to raise Isanwayo? Do you want to wipe out all your enemies?'

'How do you know of Isanwayo?' Mowende asked, some of the defiance gone from his voice.

'The same way I know about you, Mowende,' Pearson told him.

Mowende tugged hard on the girl's hair, dragging her head back. At the same time, he pressed the knife harder against her throat. The razor-sharp blade broke the flesh easily and a thin red mark appeared just below her chin.

'I will cut her heart out,' he roared.

Below, the sound of sirens was growing louder.

'It's over, Mowende,' Bishop said, taking another step forward. 'Even if you kill her.'

'You want a sacrifice?' Pearson called. 'It doesn't have to be her.' He moved closer to the parapet, his eyes never leaving the knife that Mowende held. 'Take me instead.'

69

'No.'

It was Bishop's voice that cut through the night. He looked first at the child, then at Pearson, who was still moving forward.

'If you want to kill someone then kill me, Mowende,' the journalist said. 'Let her go.'

He was now less than fifteen feet from the African, who maintained a firm grip on the child's hair. The knife was still pressed against the soft flesh of her throat.

'Let her go,' Pearson repeated, moving closer.

'What are you doing?' Bishop said. 'He'll kill her anyway.'

'No, he won't,' Pearson muttered, walking steadily towards Mowende and his captive.

'You seem very sure of that,' Mowende challenged him.

'To offer a man as a sacrifice is looked upon as

a great thing,' the journalist said. 'The spirit of a man is prized most highly. I'm right, aren't I?'

Mowende nodded slowly.

'Then take me.'

'I don't need you,' Mowende sneered.

The last word had barely left his lips when he drew the knife across the child's throat. At the same time he tugged hard on her hair, pulling her head back and stretching the flesh of her neck.

The slashed throat opened like the gills of a fish. Blood erupted from the wound, some of it spattering Pearson. The girl slumped forward as Mowende released her hair. Blood began to spread out around her body and her legs were twitching slightly.

'You bastard,' snarled Bishop.

'The child's life means nothing,' said Mowende.

'Where's the boy?' Pearson asked.

'He is dead too,' Mowende answered. 'He was dead before you even arrived here.'

'You're finished, Mowende,' Bishop rasped, advancing towards him.

Mowende took a step backward, towards the parapet of the roof.

'It's a two hundred foot fall,' Bishop reminded him. 'But if that's how you want to go, that's fine with me.'

The African merely looked at the detective and smiled, the long knife still clutched in his hand.

Pearson took his chance.

He leapt at Mowende, throwing his weight into the African, who brought the knife round in a wide arc.

The blade sheared through the top of Pearson's right arm, slicing effortlessly through muscle and scraping bone as it laid the limb open. Blood burst from the wound and sprayed into the air, some of it splashing Mowende who hissed something unintelligible under his breath.

Despite the pain, Pearson grabbed at the African's hand, trying to hold his wrist. Trying to keep the knife away from himself. For a moment he thought he was gaining the advantage, until his foot slipped in the dead girl's blood and he fell.

Bishop rushed forward, but the tall African swung the knife again and caught him across the face with a cut that split his flesh from hairline to chin. The large blade missed his left eye by a fraction, tearing his cheek open and leaving a flap of skin dangling from his face like badly hung wallpaper.

Mowende took a couple of steps backward, swiping wildly with the knife once again. Seeing his chance, Pearson drove his fist upward as hard as he could, slamming it into the African's testicles with tremendous force.

Bishop made a grab for the tall man's arm, attempting to stop him using the knife, and Mowende's next frenzied slash took off one of the detective's fingers, the digit spinning into the air, propelled by a gout of blood.

However, the African's momentum unbalanced him and Pearson managed to scramble to his feet. He kicked out again and once more caught Mowende in the groin. The big man doubled up with pain and Pearson struck at him again. The blow caught him on the top of the head and sent him tumbling backwards.

He rolled over less than five feet from the edge of the roof, the knife falling from his hand.

Bishop leapt for the knife and managed to grab it but Mowende stamped down hard on his outstretched hand. The crack of breaking bones was audible, and with a shout of pain the detective let the knife slip from his grasp.

Mowende reached for the blade and grabbed it just as Pearson slammed into him. The impact sent both men hurtling closer to the edge of the roof.

Mowende whipped the blade up before him but Pearson grabbed the sharpened steel with both hands and gripped it.

The blade sliced easily through his palms but he held on, pushing Mowende towards the precipitous drop just behind him.

Blood poured down Pearson's arms and he realised he was beginning to lose feeling in his hands as Mowende twisted the blade in a frantic effort to drag it free.

Bishop staggered nearer, blood running freely from the cut on his face and the stump of his finger. Mowende saw him and roared furiously as, with one last surge of strength, he pulled the knife away from Pearson. He struck sideways with it, driving it into the detective's stomach.

Bishop felt his mouth fill with blood as the blade tore through his intestines, cutting through them like wire through wax.

He grabbed Mowende by the throat and pushed.

The African roared in rage and fear as he felt his footing go from under him and, in the split second before they both went over the edge, he saw the triumphant look in the detective's eyes.

'No,' Pearson shouted, grabbing at Bishop's jacket.

It was useless.

For interminable seconds, Bishop and Mowende, still locked together, seemed to hang in empty air. Then they fell.

Pearson dropped to his knees, weak from pain and loss of blood.

Two hundred feet below, the bodies of Victor Mowende and Detective Sergeant Martin Bishop lay in a spreading pool of blood.

Pearson looked down at them and groaned. The sound, like the sirens below, was carried away on the wind.

70

Nick Pearson lay still inside the ambulance, aware of the pain in his right arm and both his palms.

There were two paramedics in the back of the emergency vehicle with him, one watching a saline drip that was feeding clear fluid into Pearson's left arm, while the other worked expertly to tend to the wound in his right. The journalist felt light-headed, and he knew he'd lost a lot of blood.

'Not far to the hospital now,' the first paramedic said reassuringly. 'Christ, that's deep.' He was gazing at the savage wound in the top of the newsman's arm.

The ambulance rounded a corner at terrific speed, siren screaming. Both paramedics almost over-balanced as the vehicle sped on.

'There's no damage apart from the cuts to the hands and this arm, is there?' the second man asked.

His companion shook his head, scanning Pearson's torso.

'Any other wounds that you know of?' the second man went on, addressing Pearson.

'No,' the journalist croaked, closing his eyes.

The first man checked his watch.

'We'll be at the hospital in two minutes,' he said reassuringly. 'You stay awake for me.'

Pearson wanted to comply but he felt too tired. He turned his head to one side.

'You said there were no other wounds. What about those?' the second paramedic enquired, pointing.

'No,' said his companion. 'They're scars.'

There were three small crosses in the flesh at the base of Nick Pearson's skull.

'I count religion but a childish toy, And hold there is no sin but ignorance.'

Christopher Marlowe

EXTRAS

www.orbitbooks.net

About the Author

Shaun Hutson is a bestselling author of horror fiction and has written novels under nine different pseudonyms. He was one of eight bestselling authors taking part in the BBC's End of Story competition and has appeared in his first film. He lives and writes in Buckinghamshire with his wife and daughter and two pairs of Michelle Pfeiffer's shoes.

For more details on Shaun Hutson and his books visit www.shaunhutson.com

Find out more about Shaun Hutson and other Orbit authors by registering for the free monthly newsletter at www.orbitbooks.net

An interview with

SHAUN HUTSON

Did the idea for *Unmarked Graves* come to you fully realised or did you have one particular starting point from which it grew?

It came from one idea and I expanded it. Every book I've ever written has come about like that. I think *Unmarked Graves* went through more changes than any novel I've ever written. The ideas I originally wanted to explore ended up disappearing in successive re-writes but the racism thing was there from the beginning.

How does it compare to your other novels?

For what it's worth, I like to try and do something different in each novel and it contained an idea and themes I hadn't tackled before. I'd never done voodoo before so it was something new for me. I don't like to keep recycling the same idea over and over again in a different guise. That's cheating your readers and I'd never do that.

Have you always wanted to write novels, or did the desire suddenly strike you one day?

The desire struck me after reading a novel so truly appalling I thought I had a good chance of getting published myself. That was when I was eighteen. It's a bit worrying now because when people write to me and say 'I read one of your novels and thought I'd like to write,' I usually think, 'Oh, hell, is it for the same reasons I started?'

Do you have a set writing routine and if so, what is it?

Writing is just a job like any other so I try (or did in the past) to have set hours every day. I try to write from about ten in the morning until two in the afternoon. As long as I get about three thousand words a day written it doesn't matter if it takes an hour or five hours but I NEVER work at weekends . . .

Do you feel that the horror genre has fluctuated in popularity over the last decade? Or do you think that horror fiction will always have a loyal audience?

I think that the horror genre has been free-falling into oblivion since about 1992 when *Silence of the Lambs* became such a massive success. Traditional horror as it was in the 80s is gone and will never return thanks to the massive amount of serial killer novels being published. Nothing, no matter how horrific, dreamed up by a horror writer can ever equal a human monster. As long as so many crime novels are published then horror will continue to fade as a genre. This is sad because readers, mine in particular, are amazingly loyal and, as the years progress, they are having less and less to choose from. All I can do, personally, is to thank the people who buy my books year in and year out.

Do you see any particular trends in recent horror novels?

I wouldn't know because I don't read fiction, especially not horror. I can only hope that the paucity of ideas and originality that has afflicted horror in films is not reflected in the written side of it. From what I can see glancing around bookshops however, it seems that vampires are the only thing anyone wants to read about in horror fiction. Something else I can't see changing in the near future either.

Do you ever feel the need to censor your own ideas at times?

No. I've been censored in the past over what were felt to be extreme ideas or scenes but I just write realistically and have never felt the need to curb my enthusiasm when it comes to describing scenes of violence, sex or any other kind of depravity or outrage. If readers don't like it then they can always put the book down and, to be honest, if someone picks up a book from the horror section in the first place then they should know they're not getting Enid Blyton.

You explore race in *Unmarked Graves*, obviously a very sensitive subject, did you find this difficult?

Someone somewhere is going to be offended by stuff I write so race is no different. I think that all fiction should be honest and that's what I am when I'm writing. I describe characters, situations, violence, sex, language and attitudes honestly and it doesn't matter if some of those issues happen to be contentious. They still have to be confronted.

Is there a theme that you haven't yet explored that you would like to one day?

There are still ideas that I'd like to write about. Themes remain fairly constant. To me, the book is about an idea. What the story is about and what the book means to me are two different things. I'm usually more interested in the characters; the plot and situation just carry them along. I focus on the characters, the readers focus on the plots.

If it's not an unfair question, which characters do you find most interesting and why?

Every character's interesting for different reasons. Obviously the central characters are going to mean more to me because they've got more of me in them but sometimes you end up putting bits of yourself in peripheral characters too. You just can't help it, well, I can't anyway.

Do you read mainly horror yourself, or do you like to take a rest after a long day of blood and guts?!

If I ever read, I read non-fiction. Film books, history books and stuff like that. I haven't read horror for years. If I want to see horror I'll watch the news . . .

You're obviously a film fan, having starred in two flicks yourself! Do you find yourself heavily influenced by cinema?

Films have always been a huge influence on me, mainly for the way I write. I think that it's easier to get across someone's character in a few lines of dialogue rather than by waffling on for five pages. I love the experience of the cinema, even if 90% of what's on offer these days is brainless and instantly forgettable. I love films from the seventies and earlier. At least films in those days were made because the scripts were good or because the subject matter was interesting, not like today when films are intended as star vehicles or to showcase special effects. Cinema today is as bereft of ideas and originality as it's ever been and the future looks even bleaker. When films are being made because they're based on video games then you know the industry is in a bad way. I had some great fun appearing in the films I've been in but my own books will never be filmed because they're not Hollywood friendly (i.e. full of dumb American teenagers queuing up to get slaughtered by a masked killer/alien monster/flesh eating disease/uninhabited cabin in the woods etc. etc.) . . .

Leading on from the previous question, if *Unmarked Graves* was ever filmed, who would you like to see directing and acting in it?

Whenever film rights are sold, any author should accept that what ends up on screen will bear little resemblance to what they've written so, if Paramount rang me tomorrow to say that they were going to pay me an obscene amount of money and then make *Unmarked Graves* into a musical starring Madonna, John Travolta and Amanda Bynes then I'd be delighted. In fact, if all my books were filmed I wouldn't care how they turned out as long as I'd been ridiculously overpaid for the rights . . . The reason being that no one is dumb enough to think that a bad film happens because of a bad book. The public are too clever for that.

Being a musician as well as an author, do you ever feel that your musical creativity feeds your writing or vice versa?

I play music for pleasure, I write for a living. The two are completely separate. I used to listen to rock music for half an hour before I started writing every morning to get myself hyped up but that was the extent of the cross-over.

What aspect of writing do you find most satisfying?

I used to love the excitement of starting a new novel, of sharing a new idea. Now, it's nice to get feedback from readers. As long as my readers enjoy my books then that's great. I've never cared what critics think about them (which is probably just as well), the only people who matter are the people who buy the books. There's very little reason to write otherwise.

If you enjoyed
UNMARKED GRAVES,
look out for

ALREADY DEAD

by

Charlie Huston

I smell them before I see them. All the powders, perfumes and oils the half-smart ones smear on themselves. The stupid ones just stumble around reeking. The really smart ones take a Goddamn shower. The water doesn't help them in the long run, but the truth is, nothing is gonna help them in the long run. In the long run they're gonna die. Hell, in the long run they're already dead.

So this pack is half-smart. They've splashed them-selves with Chanel No. 5, Old Spice, whatever. Most folks just think they have a heavy hand at the personal scent counter. I close my eyes and inhale deeper, because it could just be a group of bridge and tunnelers in from Jersey or Long Island. But it's not. I take that second breath and sure enough, there it is underneath: the sweet, subtle tang of something not quite dead. Something freshly rotting. I'm betting they're the ones I'm looking for. And why wouldn't they be? It's not like these things are thick on the ground. Not yet. I walk a little farther down Avenue A and stop at the sidewalk window of Nino's, the pizza joint on the corner of St. Marks.

I rap on the counter with the ring on my middle finger and one of the Neapolitans comes over.

—Yeah?

—What's fresh?

He looks blank.

—The pizza, what's just out of the oven?

—Tomato and garlic.

—No way, no fucking garlic. How 'bout the broccoli, it been out all day?

He shrugs.

—Fine, give me the broccoli. Not too hot, I don't want to burn the roof of my mouth.

He cuts a slice and slides it into the oven to warm up. I could eat the tomato and garlic if I wanted to. It's not like the garlic would hurt me or anything. I just don't like the shit.

While I wait I lean on the counter and watch the customers inside the joint. The usual crowd for a Friday night: couple drunk NYU kids, couple drunk greasers, a drunk squatter, two drunk yuppies on an East Village adventure, a couple drunk hip-hoppers, and the ones I'm looking for. There are three of them standing around the far corner table: an old-school goth chick, and two rail-thin guys, with impossibly high cheekbones, that have fashion junkie written all over them. The kind of guys who live in a squat but make the fashion-week scene by virtue of the skag they bring to the parties. Just my favorite brand of shitdogs all in all.

—Broccoli.

The Neapolitan is back with my slice. I hand him three bucks. The goth and the fashion junkies watch the two NYU kids stumble out the door. They push their slices around for another minute, then follow. I sprinkle red pepper flakes on my slice and take a big bite, and sure enough it's too hot and I burn the roof of my mouth. The pizza jockey comes back and tosses my fifty cents change on the counter. I swallow, the molten cheese scorching my throat.

—I told you not too hot.

He shrugs. All the guy has to do all day is throw slices in the oven and take them out when they're ready. Ask for one not too hot and you might as well be requesting coq au vin. I grab my change, toss the slice back on the counter and take off after the junkies and the goth chick. Fucking thing had garlic in the sauce anyway.

The NYU kids have crossed the street to cut through Tompkins Square before the cops shut it down at midnight. The trio lags behind about eight yards back, walking past the old water fountain with *Faith, Hope, Temperance, Charity* carved in the stone above it. The kids reach the opposite side of the park and keep heading east on Ninth Street, deeper into Alphabet City. Great.

This block of 9th between Avenues B and C is barren, as in empty of everyone except the NYU kids, their trailers and me.

The junkies and the goth pick up the pace. I stroll. They're not going anywhere without my seeing it. What they want to do takes a bit of privacy. Better for me if they get settled someplace where they feel safe, before I move in.

They're right on the kids now. They move into a dark patch under a busted streetlamp and spread out, one on either side of the kids and one behind. There's a scuffle, movement and noise, and they all disappear. Fuck.

I jog up the street and take a look. On my left is an abandoned building. It used to be a Puerto Rican community center and performance space, before that it was a P.S. Now it's just condemned.

I follow the scent up the steps and across the small courtyard to the graffiti-covered doors. They've been chained shut for a few years, but tonight the chain is hanging loose below the hacksawed hasp of a giant Master lock. Looks like they prepped this place in advance of their ambush. Looks like they may be a little more than half-smart.

I ease the door open and take a look. Hallway goes straight for about twelve yards then hits a T intersection. Dark. That's OK. I don't mind the dark. The dark is just fine. I slip in, close the door behind me and take a whiff. They're here, smells like they've been hanging out for a couple days. I hear the first scream and know where to go. Up to the intersection, down the hall to the right, and straight to the open classroom door.

One of the NYU kids is facedown on the floor with the goth chick kneeling on his back. She's already shoved her knife through the back of his neck, killing him. Now she's trying to jam the blade into his skull so she can split it open. The junkie guys stand by, waiting for the piñata to bust.

The other kid has jammed himself in a corner in the obligatory pool of his own fear-piss. His eyes are rolling around and he's making the high-pitched noise that people make when they're so scared they might die from it. I hate that noise.

I hear something crunchy.

The chick has the knife in. She gives it a wrenching twist and the dead kid's skull cracks open. She claws her fingers into the crack, gets a good grip and pulls, tearing the kid's head open like a piece of rotted fruit. A pomegranate. The junkies edge closer as she starts scooping out clumps of brain. Too late for that kid, so I wait a couple seconds more, watching them as they start to eat, and listening to the other kid's moaning go up another octave. Then I do my job.

It takes me three silent steps to reach the first one. My right arm loops over his right shoulder. I grab his face with my right hand while my left hand grips the back of his head. I jerk sharply clockwise, pulling up at the same time. I feel his spinal cord tear and drop him, grabbing the second one's hair before the first one hits the ground. The chick is getting up off the kid's corpse, coming at me with the knife. I punch the second junkie in the throat and let him drop. It won't kill him, but he'll stay down for a second. The chick whips the knife in a high arc and the tip rakes my forehead. Blood oozes from the cut and into my eyes.

Whatever she was before she got bit, she knew a little about using a knife, and still remembers some of it. She's hanging back, waiting for her pal to get up so they can take me together. I measure the blank glaze in her eyes. Yeah, there's still a little of her at home. Enough to order pizza and pick out these kids as marks, enough to cut through a lock, but not enough to be dangerous. As long as I'm not stupid. I step in and she thrusts at me with the knife. I grab the blade.

She looks from me to the knife. I'm holding it tightly, blood spilling out between my clenched fingers. The dim light in her eyes gets minutely brighter as something gives her the word: she's fucked. I twist the knife out of her hand, toss it in the air and catch it by the handle. She turns to run. I grab the back of her leather jacket, step close and jam the knife into her neck at the base of her skull, chopping her medulla in half. I leave the knife there and let her drop to the floor. The second junkie is just getting back up. I kick him down, put my boot on his throat and stomp, twisting my foot back and forth until I hear his neck snap.

I kneel and wipe my hand on his shirt. My blood has already coagulated and the cuts in my hand have stopped bleeding, likewise the cut in my forehead. I check the bodies. One of the guys is missing a couple teeth and has some lacerations on his gums. Looks like he's been chewing someone's skull. Probably it belonged to the clown I took care of a couple days ago, the one with the hole in his head who tipped me off to this whole thing. Anyway, his teeth aren't what I'm interested in.

Both guys have small bites on the backs of their necks. The bite radius and size of the tooth marks make me take a look at the girl's mouth. Looks like a match. Figure she bit these two and infected them with the bacteria. Happens that way sometimes. Generally a person gets infected, the bacteria starts chewing on their brain and pretty soon they're reduced to the simple impulse to feed. But sometimes, before they reach that point, they infect a few others. They take a bite, but don't eat the whole meal if you get me. No one really knows why. Some sob sisters would tell you it's because they're lonely. But that's bullshit. It's the bacteria compelling them, spreading itself. It's fucking Darwin doing his thing.

I check the girl's neck. She infected the others, but something infected her first. The bite's been marred by the knife I stuck in her, but it's there. It's bigger than the others, more violent. In fact, there are little nips all over her neck. Fucking carrier that got her couldn't decide if it wanted to just infect her or eat her. Whatever, all the same to me. Except it means the job isn't done yet. Means there's a carrier still out there. I start to stand up. But something else; a smell on her. I kneel next to her and take a whiff. Something moves behind me.

The other NYU kid. Right, forgot about him. He's trying to dig his way through the wall. I walk over to him. I'm just about to pop him in the jaw when he does the job for me and passes out. I look him over. No bites. Now normally I wouldn't do this, but I lost a little blood and I never got to eat my pizza, so I'm pretty hungry. I take out my works and hook the kid up. I'll only take a pint. Maybe two.

The phone wakes me in the morning. Why the hell someone is calling me in the morning I don't know, so I let the machine get it.

—*This is Joe Pitt. Leave a message.*

—Joe, it's Philip.

I don't pick up the phone, not for Philip Sax. I close my eyes and try to find my way back to sleep.

—Joe, I think maybe I got something if ya can pick up the phone.

I roll over in bed and pull the covers up to my chin. I try to remember what I was dreaming about so I can get myself back there.

—I don't wanna bug ya, Joe, but I figure ya gotta be in. It's ten in the morning, where ya gonna be?

Sleep crawls off into a corner where I can't find it and I pick up the damn phone.

—What do you want?

—Hey, Joe, busy last night?

—I was on a job, yeah. So what?

—I think ya made the news, is all.

Shit.

—The papers?

—NY1.

Fucking NY1. Fucking cable. Can't do shit in this city without them poking a reporter into it.

—What'd they call it?

—Uh, *Gruesome quadruple homicide.*

—Shit.

—Looks pretty sloppy, Joe.

—Yeah, well, there weren't a lot of options.

—Uh-huh, sure, sure. What was it?

—This thing I'm working on, brain eaters.

—Zombies?

—Yeah, shamblers. I hate the Goddamn things.

—You get 'em all?

—There's a carrier.

—Carrier huh? Fucking shamblers, huh, Joe?

—Yeah.

I hang up.

It's not like I didn't know leaving the bodies over there could cause trouble, I just thought they'd sit till I could clean things up tonight. Now the neighborhood's gonna be crawling with cops. But that's the least of my worries just now, because the phone is ringing again, and I sure as shit know who it's gonna be this time.

Uptown. They want me to come uptown. Now. In broad daylight. I put on the gear.

In winter this is easy, just wrap up head to toe, pull on a ski mask and some sunglasses and go. I'm not saying it's comfortable, but it's easy and you stay inconspicuous. I'll be OK once I get to the subway, but it's four blocks from here to there, and once I get uptown it'll be another few blocks to their offices. It's those blocks between the subway stations and the front doors I worry about.

I know a guy wears a white delivery-boy outfit with white latex gloves, a big wide-brimmed white cowboy hat, and zinc oxide all over his face. It keeps him pretty well covered, but even in Manhattan he gets looks. Me, I use a burnoose.

I pull on the boots, baggy pants and shirt, then the robe. The headpiece always gives me fits and I have to relearn how it wraps every time I do this.

Once it's on and feels like it won't unravel and fall off, I slip on white cotton gloves, draw the veil across my face, put on my shades and head out. Sure I get eyeballed a bit, but who gives a fuck, no one can see my face.

What I do care about is getting to First and 14th fast as I can. Even with all this cover, even with it being white and reflecting the sunlight, even though it's only four fucking blocks, I'm still getting the shit burned out of me by the short-wave UVs. And this isn't like the cuts I got last night that close right up and are gone in the morning. This hurts like hell and is gonna take days to heal. And if a patch of bare skin should happen to get hit by some direct rays? Well, I just need to be careful that doesn't happen. So I walk fast and think about aloe and ice-water baths while my skin gets roasted and my eyes tear up behind my shades and I make it to the station and rush down the steps to the sweltering, but dark platform.

The uptown guys are making a point. They could say what they need to say on the phone. They could wait for dark to rip me a new asshole, but they want to make me burn a little. They want to flex and teach me a lesson for getting sloppy. That's what's on the surface anyway. The real reason they're doing it this way is because I still haven't joined the Coalition. And the truth is, I haven't joined exactly because of shit like this. But I did get sloppy last night, and someone is gonna swing for it. So I'll fry a little to keep them happy and to keep myself alive. Because I don't want to die. Except, oh yeah, I'm already dead.

They have this building on 85th between Madison and Fifth. Nice piece of real estate. One of those anonymous brownstones that could be a consulate building or a discreet plastic surgeon's office. And, hey, right around the corner from the Guggenheim and the Met. Everything you want to know about these guys you can tell from the address: old, traditional, wealthy, powerful, and no fun at all.

I take the three steps up to the front door and press the button set in brass right next to the security camera.

—Yes?

—Pitt.

—Who?

—Joe Pitt. I have an appointment.

There's a pause and I slide into the sliver of shade available in the doorway.

—I'll need to see your face, Mr. Pitt.

—Are you kidding?

—I need to confirm your identity, Mr. Pitt.

This is choice. This is fucking brilliant. I hold the robe up over my head to shade my face and use my free hand to pull the veil quickly aside. I can feel the burn scorch my cheek and chin. I'll be bright red for a few days until it peels.

—Thank you, Mr. Pitt.

The door buzzes and I push it open and step into the foyer. It's a hardwood-and-muted-colors kind of a place. The weasel that made me strip is sitting at the security desk. I'd like to say that he's big, but that's just not the case. I'm big. This guy left big several workouts ago and has been living in huge ever since. He comes out from around the desk and looms at me.

—Sorry about the inconvenience, Mr. Pitt. May I take your things?

I pull off the robe and the headpiece and he takes them over to a coatrack while I check out my face in a mirror by the door. Yeah, I can see myself in the mirror, big deal. My face is a little pink just from being out, but there's a violent red streak across it from pulling open the veil. I can already see where the skin is turning white and flaking. It hurts like fuck. The steroid king comes back over and looks at my face.

—Hmm. I could get you something for that if you like. Some unguent or Bactine perhaps?

I stare at him.

—What happened to the guy used to be here?

—I'm sorry?

—What happened to the guy used to be here that knew who I was and didn't need to see my face?

—Oh, him.

The giant walks over to his desk and sits down so that he's back on eye level with me.

—He was executed.

No playful euphemisms around here, boy. No. He *was retired* or *dismissed*. Just get it out there. *He fucked up so we dragged him outside and staked his hands and feet to the ground and waited for the sun to come up and burn him dead from advanced skin cancer in about twenty minutes*. How do I know they did it that way? I said they were traditionalists. That's the way traditionalists do it.

—Too bad, he was alright.

Big boy just watches me.

—So any chance I can get in for my appointment? It's a really beautiful day out there and I want to make the most of it before it gets cloudy.

The giant picks up a phone and presses a button.

—He's here. I did. Thank you, sir.

He places the phone back in its cradle and points at the door across the foyer.

—Just up the stairs and to the right.

—Thanks.

I walk to the door and he presses a button on his desk to buzz it open. I stand there holding the door and turn back to him.

—Hey, who they got me seeing anyway?

—Mr. Predo will be meeting with you today, Mr. Pitt. Just up the stairs and to your right.

—Yeah, thanks.

I step through the door and let it swing shut behind me. Dexter Predo. Fuck. Predo is the head of the Coalition's secret police, and party chairman all rolled into one. He's the guy keeps everybody in line. He's the guy in charge of staking people out in the sun.